THE AUTARCH'S HEIR

JO GRAHAM

PRAISE FOR JO GRAHAM

Graham's saga of *The Calpurnian Wars* is a perfect escape, everything I want when I pick up a space opera: characters to care about, a high-stakes plot, thrilling space battles, and a good admixture of politics and behind-the-scenes diplomacy.
—K.V. Johansen, author of *Blackdog*

PRAISE FOR *FORTUNE'S FAVOR*

Fortune's Favor continues to develop and deepen the space opera world Graham introduced to us in *Sounding Dark* and *Warlady*, // a vivid canvas for Graham's penchant and skill for rich cultural details and complex societies that reminded me of Bronze Age Phoenician city states. Combine this with characters from the first two novels in the series, and new ones, and Graham shows how she's grown her world organically in this latest volume with a compelling story grounded in the very real and present desires and motivations of her creations.
—Paul Weimer, SFF book reviewer and Hugo finalist

Familiar faces to the rescue as Graham gives us a new world to fall in love with and then immediately get incredibly concerned over.
—E.K Johnston, #1 New York Times Bestselling Author

PRAISE FOR *WARLADY*

Graham skillfully combines a murder mystery, political intrigue, and space combat in the intricate and thrilling second Calpurnian Wars space opera (after *Sounding Dark*). // Graham fashions an elaborate and fascinating world, complete with complex history, religion, and politics, without ever sacrificing the plot's forward momentum. This polished page-turner should hook any sci-fi fan.
— *Publishers Weekly*

Thrilling battles in space, a murder mystery, a forbidden romance, and mature characters working to change their world, all set within another of Graham's fascinating cultures in her Nine Worlds, where far-future space opera meets spirituality with the flavour of classical antiquity—*Warlady* is a worthy sequel to *Sounding Dark,* and a story that leaves one feeling ultimately hopeful that maybe humans can after all find their way towards making a better future.

    — K.V. Johansen, author of *Gods of the Caravan Road*

PRAISE FOR *SOUNDING DARK*

Faith, luck, and grit propel this ambitious space opera from Graham (*Black Ships*). // Graham amps up the action, constructs a rich mythology of gods, cultures, and societies, and develops evocative characters that will make readers cheer. This pure sci-fi escape proves a fresh experience for fans who are tired of clichés.

    — *Publishers Weekly*

Jo Graham's space opera is a richly imagined narrative which uses its spectrum of relatable heroes who face overwhelming odds with drive, determination, grit, and most powerfully of all, hope. *Sounding Dark* uses these heroes to buttress a story on multiple levels: a fight against an interstellar tyranny, a search for the meaning of an unexpected survival against all reason, and the story of a lost, ancient connection to a Mystery reforged. With its inventive use of Sumerian motifs in its intriguing worldbuilding, *Sounding Dark* soars to reach a liminal place on the boundaries of science fiction and myth.

    — Paul Weimer, SFF book reviewer and Hugo finalist

Jo Graham specializes in writing gloriously epic yet deeply personal science fantasy, and *Sounding Dark* is the beginning of just my kind of saga: generational, political, magical.

    — E.K. Johnston, #1 New York Times Bestselling Author

For information, address:
Candlemark & Gleam LLC,
2523 Solstice Trail, Chapel Hill, NC 27516
mes@candlemarkandgleam.com

Library of Congress Cataloguing-in-Publication Data
In Progress

ISBNs: print 978-1-952456-35-0
ebook 978-1-952456-36-7
Cover art by Eleni Tsami
Editors: Athena Andreadis, Melissa Scott
Proofreader: Ellis Duspiva

www.candlemarkandgleam.com

CONTENTS

For Presleigh and Everley, my beloved daughters, sisters who always have each other's backs

PROLOGUE

"CAPTAIN, we have a 750 live and running," the weapons officer of *Cornelia* said calmly. The missile was too insignificant to show amid the mayhem on the forward viewscreen. There must be fifty missiles running, theirs and the enemy's. A Morriganian capital ship turned towards them, unscathed and untouched. *How was that possible*, Victoria Antisia wondered. *At this point, surely something would have gotten through countermeasures.* It was almost impossible to make sense of what was going on. There were forty ships engaged plus the orbital stations around Morrigan. They'd punched through and now the Morriganians counterattacked. Whoever their new Warlord or Warlady was, they were good.

"The flagship's identified," the comm officer said. "*Perilous* is launching all tubes."

"Don't get distracted," Antisia said. She sat forward in her command seat. "Our mission is to punch through. We're in the vanguard, as Altissimus Iulus directed." And that was a source of pride. Of course she had the vanguard. She'd joined Iulus as a fresh young aide fifteen years ago. Now she captained a capital ship. Now she led the vanguard.

The forward viewscreen showed a 900 and a pair of 500s closing on the Morriganian flagship. Surely at least one of them would get through active countermeasures and do some real damage! And yet the flagship didn't seem to be launching countermeasures at all. The missiles closed.

Lightning sprang across the void. It leapt from the Morriganian flagship, an impossible blue flash, current catching the 900 in its run, skipping to the pair of 500s, all of them detonating.

"What was that?" the first officer said incredulously.

"I have no idea," Antisia managed.

"Captain, a missile has acquired on us," the weapons officer said. "750."

"Countermeasures," Antisia said. She watched the countermeasures package launch. "Turn our nose into it," she said, but there was no time. The missile streaked straight and true toward their side. It was going to hit just forward of the midline.

Impact. The screens went blank, power flickering. The high, keen sound of the depressurizing alarm. And then the wind.

The screens over the ventilation system in the ceiling gave, air rushing upward to the holes, rushing upward to the gaping breach in the deck above. It didn't matter if doors sealed. It didn't matter if the ventilation system tried to. The ducts themselves were destroyed.

It was like sitting in a maelstrom. Everything in the command center was caught in a hurricane. One of the wallscreens came loose, slapping into the first officer as it flew, pulping him in his chair. The wind dragged at Antisia, only the belts of her chair holding her. The navigator, small and slender, was simply yanked out from under her straps, her mouth open in a soundless scream as she was bounced against the jagged hole in the ceiling and then through.

Antisia closed her eyes, holding her breath instinctively for whatever good it would do, for whatever few seconds of extra life it would give her. She held on as though muscles could bear the strain. *Void take me*, she thought. She had always known she would die in space.

The wind stopped. Somewhere, a seal had held. Somewhere on the deck above a bulkhead had closed. Around her, every alarm sounded. The lights were out, only the instrument lights for illumination. She could hold her breath no longer.

Antisia took a breath, choking. The air was thin, thin as a high mountain, but not completely gone. Systems were supposed to replenish, if they were still working. The gravity was out. The viewscreens were out. "Who's here?" Antisia managed. "Report."

There were two people capable of answering, the comm officer and the astrographer. "Here, Captain."

The command arm was under her fingers. There were no visuals, but she could pull a plot on her armscreen. They were sandwiched between Morrigan's orbital stations and their approaching fleet. Half of *Cornelia* was depressurized.

"Status report," Antisia said. Her head was swimming from lack of oxygen. "Tarn, see if you can get an environmental update." It wasn't the astrographer's duty, but he seemed to be in one piece.

His voice shook. "We have twenty-seven compartments depressurized. Eight are open to space. The ventral scrubbers are offline. The ventral reclamation tanks flash-froze and then ruptured. We still have radiant heat in the floor of this deck but the heat is off for all decks above this and starboard of the mainline."

"What do we have that's working?"

"We have main engines," the comm officer said. "We have port, forward, and aft thruster control."

"That's something," Antisia said. "Tarn, see if you can reroute any environmental systems. Meanwhile, go on supplemental oxygen." She opened the compartment under her chair, pulling out the mask and its small tank. She hated to use it because it only held thirty minutes supply, but if she didn't get her head clear, nothing else would matter.

"Captain."

Antisia fixed the mask in place, taking a measured breath. Don't gulp. That would cause more damage. Her swimming head cleared.

"We have a general withdrawal signal," the comm officer said. He sounded incredulous. He keyed it on speaker, Iulus' voice unmistakable. "All ships, disengage! Jump as you are able. Repeat, all ships disengage! Jump when you are able."

"He doesn't say where to jump to," Tarn said.

"Anywhere," Antisia said grimly. She knew a rout when she saw one. And there was the plot, but how to get out of this gravity soup? Her hands were shaking. It was hard to use the board. How? There must be an avenue. How? She saw her hands as though they weren't her own. And there was the track, a sling around Morrigan's light side into the space between Morrigan and the system primary. There was enough room to run up for a jump without interference. The inner planets were on the other side of the primary. There was just enough room. "Setting a new course," Antisia said. She turned *Cornelia*'s nose toward the gap, the big ship sluggish but responding.

A frigate fell in behind them, seeing the same opening. Behind them, the flagship had been cut in half by fire, each end swinging crazily. The Morriganians closed like a hunting fish pack, dark against the stars, lit by impossible flares of lightning here and there.

"Run," Antisia said quietly. "Run."

Morrigan's cities were bright against the darkside, an orbital station firing on a frigate. The frigate turned, following them as well, thrusters firing unevenly.

"I have a jump plot," Tarn said. He didn't look at the officer dead in the seat beside him. "To an intermediate point eight light years away."

"We'll take it," Antisia said. "Send it to the frigates if that's possible."

"Confirmed," the comm officer said. "It's the greatest defeat in a generation," he said quietly.

Antisia didn't even feel it. They ran sunward, mayhem behind.

CHAPTER
ONE

SIX MONTHS LATER

THE EARLY SPRING snow was falling in fat flakes past the many-paned glass doors, the twilight deepening, and Sura laid aside the broom she had used to sweep the floor around the statue. She took a long breath, looking up at it. It stood on a low stone plinth in the middle of the square chamber, unadorned and unpainted wood, save that it was blackened to charcoal on one side. The Shrine had burned eighty years ago. The image had been saved, but not without damage. The Lord of the Dance stared into the middle distance, his harp beneath his arm, half of his face charred away with the arm that would have plucked the strings. He faced the back of the chamber, the solid doors that led to the anteroom. Sura bowed to his Bright Face and walked around the statue.

It had been carved from a single piece of wood, two sides and two faces. The other face looked out through the glass doors to the terrace and beyond it to the estuary and the distant lights of Tranquility. Unscathed, it was a beautiful and stern face, his spear in his hand and his hound at his side, the Dark Face of the Lord of the Dance, the Bringer of Justice. Sura closed her eyes. "My dear Lord," she whispered. "Do not let me fail here at the test." There was no sound save the heavy plopping of snow dripping from the roof tiles.

Sura went to the double doors, her red skirts trailing against the floor she had just swept and opened them enough to pass through. It was cold. The ancient apple tree that clung to the terrace had snow sticking to its branches, but unless it iced it wouldn't hurt the buds. What was merely spring rain in Tranquility often fell as snow at this altitude. Beneath the terrace, fir trees clung to the rocky slope. Across the estuary, red lights showed among the others on the mountainside, beacons for starships incoming to Tranquility, glowing amid a golden haze of pollution clinging to the deep valley. Sura fed the fire in the stone basin. It did not gutter. There was little wind, just the slow fall of heavy flakes, each one turning and turning as they fell.

There was the sound of an electric engine, her acolyte's three-wheeler turning into the narrow lane that ran up to the back of the Shrine from the road. Sura's heart beat faster. She schooled her face to impenetrable calm, arranging the medallion that hung down onto her forehead, the gold heavy against her skin. She stood by the fire, her hands in her opposite crimson sleeves, the only bright thing besides the fire against the snow.

The rear door to the chamber opened, her acolyte coming in accompanied by a young man. He was thirty or so, lean and tall, his curling black hair cropped close in the Calpurnian fashion, a little mustache above his full lips. He wore a dark coat against the snow, and his eyes looked around the Shrine curiously, stopping on the burned face of the god. He said something Sura could not hear through the door. Her acolyte answered.

She knew the moment he saw her. She saw his eyes widen just a little. But of course he did not know her. He simply saw the priestess standing in the snow, white hair making a headdress of many braids, her gown as red as blood.

Her acolyte slid open the doors. "I have brought Bel Alan, my lady."

Sura inclined her head. "Be welcome, Bel Alan," she said as he came through the doors onto the snowy terrace.

"Thank you." He was looking around curiously, taking in everything at a glance. "I'm honored, but I have no idea why you wanted to see me."

Sura nodded to the acolyte, who made a slight bow as she withdrew to set the tea in an internal room. "Make the offering with me."

"If you like." He looked perplexed. "But I don't…"

She took the applewood dipper and the bowl of resins and precious herbs. "…make offerings?" she asked. "What god do you serve?" She thought she knew the answer.

"None," he said. His eyes met hers directly. "I'm not a religious man."

Sura smiled. "If you do not believe, then it will do you no harm to simply follow a quaint local custom." She put the dipper in his hand, her hand over his, arranging his fingers on the handle as though he were a child. "There. One scoop, no more, for the Lord of the Dance who holds His hounds in check." She helped him scatter it across the flames, dried flowers burning blue for a moment before they flared out.

"Forgive me," Bel said. "But do I know you?"

"I think not," Sura said. She stepped quickly away, putting the dipper back where it belonged. "But I know of you, Bel Alan. They say you are a very clever man and capable of undertaking the most delicate deceptions."

"Is that what they say?" he murmured. Bel glanced around the terrace. "But what's that to you?"

"I find myself in need of someone to provide very specialized services," Sura said. She went to the doors. "Come inside and we will discuss them."

He followed her, of course. She went through the square chamber and through another sliding door to the right, into a room set against the edge of the terrace. The screens were open, showing night and falling snow. A little table had been set with two scarlet cushions, a steaming teapot and cups waiting. Sura sank down onto one cushion. Bel sat cross-legged on the other, reaching for his coat. "Do you mind if I take it off?"

"Of course not," Sura said. "Make yourself comfortable." He wore a loose black shirt beneath it, wide sleeves clasped tight at the wrists, half-boots that were worn and reheeled despite the polish of the leather. He was very graceful and not as young as she had imagined, but that was foolishness as she knew his age to the day.

"What's the job?" Bel asked.

Sura poured the tea. Her voice was steady. "I need someone to recover an object from inside the Viceregal Palace."

He whistled. "That's advanced."

Sura smiled as she handed him his cup. "And that is why I have contacted you. I understand you're expensive but the best."

"I am expensive. And I am the best." Bel smiled and took the cup. "Tell me more. What's the object and where is it?"

"The object is a headdress referred to as the Solaste Crown, a gift from the Morriganian Warlord to the Princess of Lono some eight hundred years ago. It was one of the treasures of the royal family until their extinction eighty years ago. It is currently in the treasury of the Viceregal Palace, an example of ancient and barbarous art." Sura smiled at him over the rim of the cup. "Needless to say, it is of considerable symbolic value to us."

"Us?"

"The people of Lono, who would see it redeemed from our conquerors." Sura returned his smile pleasantly.

Bel frowned. "That doesn't sound like the kind of thing that can just go missing and not have anybody notice. Not to mention getting into the Viceregal Palace, which other than the starship yards might be the most heavily guarded place on the planet."

"And that is why you are ideal," Sura said. She lifted her left hand to tick off the reasons on her fingers. "First, you are Calpurnian. You will not arouse suspicion as a Lonoi would. Second, you are unknown to the Viceregal Palace's current occupant, Altissima Antisia. Third, I have a plan."

Bel grinned. "I like a lady with a plan. So what is it?"

"As you know, until recently Lono was the province of the Autarch Altissimus Iulus. While he was here only rarely, he derived enormous income from Lono. And he was here more often in the past, when he was a young man. But now he is dead." She opened her hand. "Assassinated after his failure to conquer Morrigan. Antisia was a faithful deputy of his and loyal to the end. She has fallen out with Altissima

Thurinia who claims everything that was his. Antisia would be delighted to find an excuse not to turn Lono over to her. If, for example, a natural son of the Autarch were to appear and lay claim?"

Bel looked thoughtful. He took a drink of his tea, eyes sweeping shut as he drank, then looked up. "So you want me to pretend to be this natural son? There's a big problem with that. They'll pull a DNA sample in ten minutes flat and check it. The moment they see I'm lying, it's over."

"Of course they'll pull a DNA sample," Sura said. "But do you think they have the Autarch's DNA just lying around? They'll have to send your sample on a courier ship to Calpurnia for comparison, and then the response will have to be brought back. That will take five or six days. In the meantime, you can convince Antisia to allow you to stay in the Viceregal Palace and give you honors and access. That's where your cleverness comes in."

Bel took a deep breath. "So before the courier ship gets back, I steal this thing and disappear."

"Along with whatever substantial personal funds belonging to the Altissimus Iulus you have convinced Antisia to grant you access to." Sura lifted her cup. "I want the Solaste Crown. The funds are entirely yours. And of course any other valuables you remove."

Bel leaned back. "That's quite an offer."

"I need a con man who can play the Calpurnian Altissimus to the hilt," Sura said. "And you're about the same height and build as the Autarch was, dark-skinned and dark eyed. You don't look so dissimilar that it's unconvincing. I can certainly provide you with a cover story, including that you've just learned of your patrician birth. Once you're in, you've got five days, or four if you want to be safe, to get the Crown and anything else and get out."

"This is actually not crazy," Bel said.

"Indeed," Sura said. She watched him. "Are you interested?"

"I believe so," Bel said, and touched his cup to hers.

For a moment when he awoke, Bel was uncertain where he was. The warmth of the old-fashioned box bed radiated upward from the mattress cover, and the sheets and blankets smelled faintly of juniper. He had dreamed—something. It dissipated, leaving only contentedness. He had spent the night at the Shrine. Bel looked around the tiny room, one narrow window with a closed shade, a box bed built into the far wall. There were no distractions. Either this room was intended for pilgrims or people who were very serious about getting away from the rest of the world. There was no screen, no pictures or anything else. And yet he'd slept well. Like a baby in its mother's arms, the saying was. Maybe there was something to the heated bed thing.

Bel sat up, stretching, and walked over to open the shade. The window showed nothing but a strip of snowy garden, though the snow was beginning to melt, the sun coming watery through low clouds. He took a shower in the adjacent cube. There was a brick of soap, green and smelling of some herb he couldn't quite name. It made him smile.

It was with quite a sense of well-being that he emerged from his room and went in search of the priestess. It had probably been a good idea to come back to Lono. A good job, a challenging job that paid well, was a chance to turn around the streak of bad luck that had plagued him for nearly a year. Since then it had been one thing after another, one lost stake after another, one costly mistake after the next. He'd run through his currency and his welcome fast.

The room with the burned statue was quiet. Bel slipped through in stockinged feet. There was something about not wearing outdoor shoes in the Shrine, or at least he thought so. Its blank eyes followed him. It was creepy the way they'd carved it, like it was looking at you and measuring you, and that was made worse by the burns, like someone who ought to be dead watching you.

The priestess was down the hall in a techno office. Mostly techno, anyway. The floor was still bare polished wood, and there was the same narrow window to the dark bushes of the garden, but there was a desk with a big screen built into the surface, a kneeling chair with thick padding, and all the things you'd expect in an office that wasn't on Lono. It was a little surprising to see her sitting in the chair, her red robes less ornate than yesterday, though her many braids were pinned up like a white crown. She looked up when she saw him, a smile transforming her face. "Ah, Bel. I hope you slept well?"

"Yes, thank you." He stopped just inside the door.

"I have some things for you," she said. "I've been working this morning." There was a faint reproach in her voice.

Bel scrubbed his hand through his damp hair. "What time is it?"

"Nearly noon." Her mouth twitched. "I have had hours to prepare these documents for you."

"I'm sorry." Bel winced. Way to make a great impression, sleeping in like a kid! "I didn't set an alarm."

"No reason to." She passed him a reader. "Take a look at these, if you will, and tell me if you think they will suffice for your purposes."

There wasn't a second chair in the room. Bel stood while he flipped through the documents. The first was a registered certificate of birth stating that Nereus Iulus was the natural and biological child of Amari Calado and Sanius Iulus, with Bel's own birthdate filled in neatly, the creation date on the document matching the birthdate. The second was an affidavit signed by Sanius Iulus stating that Nereus Iulus was acknowledged as his son, the date twelve days later. Lastly, there was a legal document again purporting to be from Sanius Iulus leaving to his natural son, Nereus, all of his personal property and currency on the world of Lono, up to and including honors granted, "given that he is also the son of Amari Calado, a Descendant of the Sun." It was dated four months later, the date verified by document creation and download.

Bel looked up with a respectful nod. "These are good work," he said. "Very convincing. You have good people."

"Yes," the priestess said. "I do." She glanced down at her screen, frowning at something she saw there. "Can you work with that?"

"Absolutely," he said. "I'll need a good cover story to explain where Nereus has been for the last thirty years."

"Well then," she said. "If you will take the midday meal with me, we will concoct something that seems plausible." She looked at him critically. "You don't look too dissimilar as it is. The shape of your face isn't so different from the Autarch's. You are dark as he was, and you may seem to have the Calado eyes." She began to rise, and Bel offered her his arm to help her out of the kneeling chair. She leaned on it a moment. "Do you know of the Calado?"

"Not much, madam," Bel said. Women everywhere appreciated politeness and charm whatever their age, even if it was from their employee.

"They were the Descendants of the Sun, the old dynasty of ruling Princes of Lono. Some branch or other of the Calado had ruled this world for nearly seven hundred years. I won't say all ruled well." She smiled at him sideways as they went down the hall to the room they had taken tea in the night before. It was laid for the midday meal, the silent acolyte standing by with a pitcher to pour the soup. "And that was their downfall, of course. The last Prince was lazy and far from intelligent. He was easily provoked by the Calpurnians into starting a war he could not win. Lono was crushed."

"Yes, I know that part," Bel said. He sat down on the cushion opposite her. "I'm actually half Lonoi myself."

"Are you?" She looked pleased, but there was a false note in it. Probably she already knew that.

"My mother is Lonoi," Bel said. "But she's married to a Calpurnian and they live in the Adelphi Rim. She met him when he was an enlisted soldier."

"Your father?" The priestess glanced up at the acolyte. "We will take the full meal today. I know I don't usually, but I have a guest."

"Yes, Sura," the acolyte said, and slipped out.

"No, my stepfather," Bel said. "My bio father didn't stick around."

"Ah," the priestess lifted her soup bowl, drinking the clear soup.

"So this Nereus," Bel said. "Is his mother a real person?"

"She was. She died many years ago, so she can't unfortunately reappear and mess up this plan," the priestess said. "She was from one of the cadet lines of the Calado, and her mother survived the disaster eighty years ago, so she had a claim to the Principate. But she's long dead."

Bel frowned. "So you've written it that Nereus is royal?"

"It has to be convincing that she is someone Sanius Iulus would find important enough to acknowledge a son with," she said. "He certainly wouldn't acknowledge a child by some serving girl. Too plebian."

"No," Bel agreed. "Well, that works for me. As long as there aren't a bunch of long-lost aunts popping out of the curtains that I'm supposed to recognize."

"There is no one on Lono who you could possibly be expected to recognize," the priestess assured him.

"That would be hard to carry off." Bel looked up as the acolyte returned with baskets of steaming rolls. "If it's just creating a persona, it's best to stick to lies that are mostly true. If nobody knows anything about this Nereus, I'll say I grew up on Adelphi so that I can talk about it convincingly."

"It is indeed best to stick to lies that are mostly true," the priestess said with a smile. "So tell me what you intend to use as background. We will say that you found these documents among the effects of your late mother, who raised you on Adelphi in exile. Discovering them, you brought them to me to understand what they meant."

"Works for me," Bel said.

"So who is this Nereus?" the priestess asked. She looked like she was enjoying this part. "Is he married? Involved? Has children?"

"No, too complicated," Bel said. "He's the kind of guy who never settles down. There's always something else out there, someone fascinating right around the corner. It's a big galaxy. What's the point of limiting yourself? He's got a lot going on."

"What's his education? Did he go to the university on Calpurnia?"

"He dropped out," Bel said promptly. "He's not good at conforming. At fitting into a tiny little slot so he can live in a tiny little box with tiny little people."

The priestess' smile grew. "A man with ambition. Curious. Clever."

"Yeah, maybe so," Bel said. "But Calpurnia's no place for a man with ambition, unless he's a patrician."

"But now Nereus is," the priestess said. "So…"

Bel nodded, taking a bite of a crunchy roll. "He's in a hurry to be recognized. He wants Altissima Antisia to get this done so he can start exercising the power he's inherited."

The priestess nodded approvingly. "Not wealth?"

Bel shrugged. "Currency is worth the opportunity it buys. Or the happiness. By itself, it's just something you gamble with. Spend it, and you've got a thing, even if that thing is just a memory of an experience."

She looked startled. "You are not the mercenary I expected, Bel Alan."

"No?" He raised an eyebrow. "Besides, we're talking about Nereus."

"So we are." She lifted the soup bowl again. "Then let us finish his backstory, and I will see if I can beg an appointment with the Altissima Antisia. The afternoon is yours to do with as you like. I will ping you when I've arranged an appointment."

Golden Wanderer came out of jump just within the orbit of Lono's greater moon, screens resetting as the exterior cameras came online. The comm board pinged. "This is Lono Control. Please identify yourself."

Aurore Melian tilted her seat into the upright position, swinging the arm with its touch screen across her body. She keyed the comm on. "This is the Menaechman merchanter *Golden Wanderer* inbound for Tranquility Yards." Around her, the other three crew were locking their seats upright as well.

"What is your port of origin and your cargo?" Lono Control sounded bored at the routine questions.

"Port of Beira, Menaechmi," Aurore replied. "Top cargo on our manifest is coffee beans and textiles. Additionally, 60 percent of our hold is consigned freight on pallets to individual importers."

"Tranquility Yards, not Tranquility Port?"

"We're coming in for a refit," Aurore said. "We'll offload and go into a refit slip—Mari Brothers is doing the upgrade."

"Got you, *Golden Wanderer*," Lono Control said. "Sending your approach vector. You're cleared for Tranquility Yards dock seven."

"Affirming, Tranquility Yards dock seven," Aurore said. "Thanks, Lono Control. Seeing the vector now."

One of the two forward screens had shifted to show the approach corridor, an unusual one, but there must be a lot of traffic, coming in over the Armstrong Sea from the east, across the big island of Saetag, and then into Tranquility overland. Usually the approach was from the west, over the Northern Ocean. Lono was 90 percent ocean, its small island continents in chains across the seas from pole to pole.

"Passengers and crew leaving the yards area must go through customs," Lono Control added.

"Understood," Aurore said. She wondered if she could get a through line to the factor, but probably not. Lono usually had too much traffic and the authorities weren't terribly flexible. Well, maybe they'd at least notify. Her voice was casual. "Can I get a ping sent to Idra Melian, House Melian's factor? Just an autonotify to let her know we're inbound?"

"Sorry, you'll have to let your own factor know after landing."

"Understood," Aurore said. "Starting our approach now." Well, it would have saved time, but it wasn't critical.

Lang, in the second seat, leaned over as Aurore cut the comm. "That would be the reason," he said, nodding at the other forward screen. A Calpurnian capital ship rode in low orbit over the Northern Ocean, lines out from its crumpled bow tethering it to a tender. A frigate held geostationary position further out, its extensive battle damage clear even on long-range sensors. There might be a third one beyond it in a polar orbit. "Look at that thing. It's a wonder it's in one piece."

"Damage from Morrigan," Aurore guessed. "Want to put money on there being a couple more in Tranquility Yards? I don't think you could land that capital ship, but if there's not a frigate or two in the Yards I'll be surprised." She craned her neck as though that would somehow make the plot show more. "There weren't so many last time I was here."

"Think there's going to be any ordnance for us?" Lang asked. After all, the whole point of the refit was to equip *Golden Wanderer* with a pair of missile launchers.

"We're paying for it," Aurore said. Her father had literally yelled at the cost, but he'd agreed and they had cash upfront for the payment.

"Yeah, but will we shoot up the place if we don't get it?" Lang asked. "They run the planet. We don't."

"Money talks," Aurore said. "I can grease some palms if I need to." She shrugged. "We'll get what we need."

Lang nodded, apparently willing to trust in House Melian's purse, though Aurore was all too aware it wasn't actually bottomless. She'd rather run the ship any day than go over the books with her father, but he was determined that she was going to understand every nuance of the House's finances. "After all," he kept saying, "you're my heir and who knows what might happen?" He'd had a close call and now mortality was creeping up on him, but at least he hadn't refused to let her handle the armament. She'd been afraid he'd insist on her not going off-world, and that would be intolerable, stuck in an office with the books instead of the helm of a starship.

They were passing through a cloud layer, *Golden Wanderer*'s steering thrusters firing to slow them. Lang read off altitude and vector by routine, though she could see it plainly displayed. Slowing. Thrusters fired again. "Attitude adjustment beginning," Aurore said on the internal comm for the benefit of crew and passengers. "Artificial gravity going offline." *Golden Wanderer* tilted, nose rising, preparing to land with the engine pod down. There was a sudden, sickening drop as the gravity adjusted. Instead of facing forward, she was lying back strapped in her chair, the screens above her head rather than in front of her.

They broke through the cloud layer, the camera reorienting to show the land below, the big island dusted in snow on the mountains, the estuary silver in the dim sunlight.

"There you go, captain," Lang said. "Right on. Looks like a pair of frigates snugged in there."

Aurore was preoccupied with the landing procedure and barely spared a glance. "Bet they're in crap shape." There were the field beacons, the concentric circles that marked their zone, bright green lights visible even by day. "Starting final orientation."

Golden Wanderer tilted straight up, slowing further, easing down on its own thrust in the middle of the lit circles. Eighty meters. Twenty meters. Twelve meters. It seemed like they were barely moving.

"Touch," Aurore said, and with a jar the gear touched down. "Full engine cut."

"Cutting the main engine," Lang said.

Golden Wanderer eased down onto the field.

"Welcome to Lono, *Golden Wanderer*," Lono Control said. "Turning you over to the tow boss."

"Got it. Thanks, Lono Control," Aurore said.

"Nice landing," Lang said. "Not a bounce."

"I never bounce," Aurore said with a smile. It was a long-standing joke. She turned the internal comm back on. "We're down," she said. "Please stay strapped until the tow has us in the cradle." She could see the tow coming out, ready to take *Golden Wanderer* to its berth. This was always the tedious part, waiting for the tow to secure them and then tilt them down again, nose forward rather than up, and then pull them to the correct berth. *Golden Wanderer* was too big to dock by itself, not like a little shuttle or scoutship.

Local info was pouring in as wireless data connected to the port systems. Chilly but not cold, respiratory alert for those with pollution sensitivities, 84 percent humidity, local time 13:47 of a 26-hour day, so midday on a damp day in early spring. While the tow secured them, she sent a quick burst to Idra, the factor, to let her know *Golden Wanderer* was in, and another to Mari Brothers to let them know *Golden Wanderer* had arrived for the refit and requesting an appointment to go over the specs.

"How long is our layover, captain?" Lang asked.

"No idea yet. At least a local day to offload, though I'll need most of the crew for that. Then we'll turn her over to Mari Brothers to mount the missile launchers, which shouldn't take more than a couple of days. Load ordnance, familiarize ourselves with the new systems, and then we'll take *Golden Wanderer* home." Aurore smiled. "They'll be some time for a layover while they're mounting the launchers."

"I should think so." Another voice joined the conversation, and Aurore twisted around to see her sister standing in the command center door.

"Didn't I say to stay strapped in?" Aurore asked.

Dian Melian shrugged. "Until we tilted. But right now we're just rolling along in the tow to the dock. My screen's not showing anything useful."

"You've got the same view I do," Aurore said. She wished she hadn't had to bring her sister on this trip, but their father had insisted. *You'll need Dian for diplomacy.* That was a load of excrement. There was no diplomacy involved in a refit. He'd wanted her gone because he wasn't sure how Dian was handling Caralys's pregnancy and a business trip to Lono was a good excuse.

"Is Idra going to meet us at the dock or are we going to her office?" Dian asked.

"I don't know yet. I just pinged her."

The camera view changed as the tow turned into the lane of berths. The forward view was suddenly filled with the ship in the first berth, its enormous bulk dwarfing *Golden Wanderer*. It was a Calpurnian frigate, sleek and streamlined, paired missile tubes forward and on its ventral surface, *Impenetrable* painted on its side in letters three meters high. And yet just aft of the missile tubes, the sides were covered in scaffolding, plating removed to show compartments within. The aft thruster pod was missing, twisted struts showing where it had been taken off.

Dian took a deep breath. "Dancer, that's fucked."

Aurore nodded. "This must be the end of the battle line from Morrigan finally getting in for refit. I'm not sure how that landed with half its steering thrusters messed up."

"Maybe they had some steering and the yards have taken the pod off because it was a total loss," Dian said.

"Yeah," Aurore said. "Those look like scorch marks on the hull. See there? What could do that?"

"No idea," Dian said.

Lang looked up. "How'd you like a ship like that, captain?"

"I'd like one in better shape," Aurore said. And yet her eyes devoured the lethal shape of it.

"So a good part of the remaining Calpurnian Navy is loyal to Altissima Antisia," Dian mused.

"Where do you get that?" Aurore asked.

"They're here, aren't they? They wouldn't be berthed for a refit on

Lono if they hadn't pledged to her," Dian said. "Which means Thurinia holds Calpurnia." Aurore must have looked blank. "The one who is emerging as leader of the Social Logic faction and potential Autarch. Do you not pay any attention to politics?" Dian said impatiently.

"Not if I can help it," Aurore said.

"And Daddy wants you as House heir," Dian said.

"We are not getting into that again," Aurore said with a look that said, *not in front of the crew.*

Dian nodded. They were in agreement on that. Despite any conflicts between the mainline family, in public they presented a united front.

"Let's get docked," Aurore said.

CHAPTER
TWO

BEL ALAN THREADED his way through the narrow streets of Tranquility. The land sloped steeply down to the estuary, and all the flat land along the shore was filled with industrial buildings, the haze of chemical exhaust lying low in the valley. Above, the steep sides of the mountains were a tangle of houses and apartments clinging to the contours of the land. Some were new, Calpurnian architecture of glass and steel, sealed buildings with extraordinary views. Most were traditional however, wood and mortar, upper stories built onto older buildings beneath, wooden balconies leaning out over dizzying drops, bluish-green conifers everywhere to help hold the land in shape. Their root systems prevented landslides. It wasn't impossible for the whole mountainside to simply collapse. It had probably happened. And yet people built where they did for a variety of reasons.

Bel went on foot through the narrow streets. He'd gotten Sura's acolyte to drop him off on the theory that he needed to get his clothes from his lodging. That was true, but he had a lot more to do than that. He waited at a tram stop, the clouds lowering but not quite drizzling. If it had snowed in the city as at the Shrine, it had all melted. The tram pulled up. People piled out, old women clutching string bags, grizzled men with their lunches wrapped in waxed paper, a few younger women laughing and talking despite the drizzle, a few with small children. Older children would be at school or at work. So would everyone who worked in the vast starship yards or the factories that supplied them. That was where the good wages were.

Bel swung up on the back step after a woman with a toddler, hanging onto the handstraps. In his blue wrapped overcoat and boots he attracted no attention, looks that were not out of place on Lono, nothing in his dress or manner foreign. Bel was good at blending in. And he'd been back to Lono since he'd left as a child, though of course never to the Shrine before. His business was more often with gambling marks than religious leaders. Still, he knew his way around.

He rode the tram down the winding streets, past shops and open-fronted stick shops, the smells of their roasting vegetables and meat following him. The tram skirted the square with the open-air second-hand market, wares protected against the drizzle by red and yellow tarps. Then it turned into a steep modern street, cutting through apartments that hung over the road, straight down to the estuary shrouded in haze rising from the round tanks of the Reer Factory. They bottled liquid chemicals under pressure for starships—hydrogen, oxygen, chlorine—everything that a ship carried in a tank. Most of them were harmless. Some weren't. He vaguely remembered someone telling him about a chlorine leak at the plant that had killed a bunch of workers a few years ago, saying insouciantly that thankfully chlorine was a heavy gas and their apartment was two thousand feet up the mountainside.

Yeah. Lono was like that. They took the bad in stride and made bad jokes about it, took a flask of warm wine and drank to the Blameless Prince. Someday a huge, hulking, blessed warrior would arise from the Old Line and drive the Calpurnians away. Well, it had been eighty years they'd been waiting. They'd keep waiting, singing sad songs and working in the factories. And that was probably what Sura was up to, wasn't it? Bel thought. She wanted the Solaste Crown. It was an emblem of that dead royal house. Presumably that made it a symbol of Lonoi independence. He was happy to get it for her, but a crown doesn't change anything. Anyway, by now Lono's economy was so entwined with Calpurnia's that if every Calpurnian suddenly disappeared, everybody would starve.

Bel looked out the window at the factory gates behind their fences. Nobody was getting on or off here. It was the middle of the shift. These were the good jobs, even if they came with the inevitable religious stigma of dealing with technology. Though what was that anymore, Bel wondered, when even the Shrine had a modern datalink? Ok, it wasn't in a public part of the building, but it was there.

And sure, not every ship that was made or repaired here was Calpurnian, but without the Calpurnians and their shipyards and their heavy industry, what would people do for a living? And what about people like him, part Calpurnian and part Lonoi? His mom had moved to Adelphi when his stepfather was assigned there, but there were tens of thousands of people like him in eighty years. Were they supposed to leave? Even if they'd lived here their whole lives? What about people married to Lonoi, with Lonoi children?

Bel shook his head. Old people would teach sad songs to young-bloods who wanted a fight, but it was a foolish dream. There was no Blameless Prince, no promised one rising to save Lono. But it was probably better for the Shrine to have the crown than for it to sit in an anthropological display. And Sura had promised him everything else he managed to liberate from the Altissima, which would certainly be enough for a stake, a new start.

If the deal worked. Bel stepped down from the tram when it stopped at the main entrance to the starship yards. Sura might double-cross him. Easy enough to take the crown and the other goods too and leave him to hang out to dry with the Calpurnian authorities. He'd have to get out before the DNA test came back. No reason Sura couldn't simply delay him until it did. Then he'd be in hot water, with nothing except his word to show that the Shrine had anything to do with it. No, you never count on a client for your exit strategy. You depend on yourself.

The rain had finally stopped. Bel made his way down the line, looking up at the massive ships in dock. There was a warship that looked truly beyond repair. Well, none of the warships did him any good. He headed down the line toward the smaller ships at the end.

There was a sturdy merchanter in berth, the hull shiny and neatly painted, scaffolding underneath. Someone in a painter's mask was touching up the name on the rear hull: *Golden Wanderer*. Meanwhile, a crew was removing hull plating just aft of the center, probably to install the sleek 250 missile launcher cradled on a lift beside. A woman was scrambling around on the yellow poly nets that led from the scaffolding up onto the curve of the rear hull, cargo pants and a white shirt under a loose, worn jacket. She slid down the last ladder.

"Hey there," Bel called. "Is this your ship?"

She turned. Her dark hair was cut short, hacked off in what was supposed to be a blunt cut, but humidity had turned it into a loose mass of waves around a startlingly pretty face, pale and angular with full lips. She was his age or perhaps a couple of years younger, and she looked him up and down, apparently deciding that he wasn't an authority or someone who worked for the yards. "I'm the captain," she said. "Why?"

Bel walked over to her. "I'm looking for passage off Lono. What's your registry and where are you bound?"

"*Golden Wanderer* belongs to House Melian out of Beira on Menaechmi," she said. "We're fitting a missile launcher and then we're loading cargo and bound to our home port. We've got room for paying passengers if you don't mind not knowing exactly what our schedule is yet. We're still mounting the launcher and waiting on ordnance."

Bel held out his hand. "Bel Alan," he said. "Menaechmi sounds good. How long do you think you'll be?"

"Aurore," she said, shaking his hand firmly. "A few days? Maybe four or five? Are you flexible on your dates?"

Bel nodded. "Reasonably flexible. A week is too long, but three days, four days, five days, that's aces."

"I don't think we'll be five days," Aurore said. She took off her work gloves. "Unless something is seriously wrong. The launcher is being installed today and then there's a couple of days for systems integration and structural testing. After that, it's just restocking O2, water, flushing the systems that might have been affected by the refit—that's not big stuff."

"No," Bel said. "What's Beira like?"

She raised an eyebrow. "You want to go somewhere you know nothing about? Ever been to Menaechmi before?"

"I've been to Casera," he said. "Briefly. Different city." He shrugged. And that had been a disaster. He'd spent almost the entire time in a casino running a con which had crashed and burned. He'd been lucky to avoid arrest. However, the Cities of the Coast were all separate entities. Even if he was wanted in Casera, another city wouldn't be looking for him. And Menaechmi was certainly not on friendly terms with Calpurnia right this minute. "Nice place. Nice beaches."

"Yeah, we have those too," Aurore said. "Bigger than Casera. Older. A good bit cooler, since Beira's well north of the equator." She quirked an eyebrow at him. "Are you in some kind of trouble with the law?"

"No, but I'm planning to be," Bel said with a grin.

Aurore laughed. "Sure. If that's how you play it."

"I'll play it any way you like, beautiful one," Bel said. Menaechmen liked polish.

She didn't stop smiling. "Don't you beautiful one me," Aurore said. "I don't do charm and I don't like *hapalos*."

"Excuse me?"

She eyed the open collar of his coat. "Flowered shirt. Little mustache. Cologne. *Hapalos*. You could translate that as 'fancy man.' Not my taste."

"You mean like a gigolo?" Bel said. He raised an eyebrow suggestively. "You think I'm smoking enough to make a living on it?"

"I expect you're making a living on something I don't need to know about," Aurore said.

"You probably don't want to know," Bel said. A pretty starship captain with a sense of humor was definitely brightening his day, with extra points for verbal sparring. "Unless you like rogues."

"I absolutely do not like rogues," Aurore said. The corners of her mouth twitched like she was trying not to smile. "I like respectable, hardworking men with a solid work ethic and a serious mind."

"So do you have one?" Bel asked.

"Not at present." Aurore tilted her head. "But we were talking about passage to Menaechmi." She named a sum that was substantial but not unreasonable.

"That works," Bel said. Of course he didn't have the currency, but he would, right? "Pay you at boarding?"

"Sure," Aurore said. She did smile now. "That means if you don't show up, I leave you."

"Right." Bel grimaced. "So can you ping me a couple of hours before you lift?"

She nodded. "Where can I reach you?"

"How about if I ping your ship and give you my code?" Bel said. He'd give her his comm bracelet, but he'd rather wait until everything was surer.

She gave him a cynical look. "Yeah. Even odds whether you do or not."

"It's a passenger, not an assignation," he said with mock indignation. "Like you said, I don't show up, you raise ship without me. If I get left, it's on me."

"That's the deal then," Aurore said. "Send me your code and I'll let you know when we have a departure time."

"Absolutely," Bel said with a little bow. She shook her head and walked off toward the boarding ramp. He grinned. That had lifted his spirits. There was a lot riding on this job and it made him nervous. But now at least he had a back door that didn't depend on Sura playing straight. These were high stakes. Best to have a card of his own up his sleeve.

"You don't have any missiles?" Aurore said incredulously.

On the screen in *Golden Wanderer*'s command center, Tenn Mari shrugged. He was an Innocent, the tattoo of a leaping flame over his right eyebrow, his head shaved. "Oh, we have 'em," he said. "But I can't give them to you. The Altissima has requisitioned all missiles for the Calpurnian Navy."

"Then what in the name of the Infernal did we just pay you for?" Aurore spread her hands. "We just handed over hard currency."

"For missile launchers and their installation," Tenn Mari said. "You've got 'em."

"And the missiles!" Aurore said. "What good do you think the launchers are without any ordnance?"

"The Altissima has requisitioned all missiles for the Calpurnian Navy," Mari said. He shrugged again as if at the vicissitudes of the world.

Aurore shook her head. "So you have them, and we've paid for them, but you can't give them to us."

"Yep." Mari grimaced. "That's the way it is. I can give you a refund on the missiles."

"I don't want a refund," Aurore shouted. "I want the missiles that we paid for! That's the whole point of arming the merchanters. To have missiles!"

"Can't do it," Mari said. He shook his head. "We can't release any missiles without the express permission of the Altissima."

Dian had come in and was perched on the edge of one of the couches, making cutting motions out of sight of the camera.

"House Melian has currency. We could buy them from somebody else," Aurore pointed out.

"Nope," Mari said. "All the fitters are under the same order. And all the ordnance coming off the line. It's all supposed to go to the Navy unlessen they release it."

Dian's eyes widened, her cut motion broader.

"Fine," Aurore said. "Thanks for your time." She cut the comm. "What, Dian?"

"He can't do it," Dian said. "And he's more scared of the Calpurnians than he is of you."

"Dancer's balls, what are we supposed to do?" Aurore said. "We can't go anywhere else because we already paid for the missiles. We paid for this expensive refit. Dad's going to blow up like the Old Man if we come back without any missiles and can't do anything. He's stuck paying the Eresh pirates until we at least get a couple of merchanters armed."

"So we get the Altissima to release the missiles to us," Dian said. She crossed her legs. "We need to employ Dad-levels of charm." She looked at Aurore. "Me, not you. You don't always make a good impression."

"And you do?" Aurore huffed.

"I can be charming," Dian smirked. "Unlike you. Who will walk in and demand the Altissima give you the missiles."

"They're our missiles," Aurore said. "We paid for them."

"And we want them to defend ourselves against the Calpurnians," Dian said. "Which the Calpurnians can't be very happy about." She leaned back against the couch arm. "Yes, it's a different faction, Federationist rather than Social Logic. By all accounts, Altissima Antisia was loyal to the Autarch Iulus. She didn't recognize any authority from Altissimus Cassian and probably didn't mind a bit that the Eresh pirates killed him when he shook down Beira. But it doesn't make us look like friends. Maybe enemies of her enemy, but not friends. She's not going to let us take delivery of ordnance unless she's convinced that we're not going to use it against her."

"So you're going to talk her into it?" Aurore asked skeptically.

"Dad-levels of charm," Dian said.

"It's not going to work."

"If it doesn't work, what have we lost?" her sister asked. "We don't have missiles now. We don't have missiles then. But if it does work, then I convince her to release our ordnance and we go our merry way."

"Fine," Aurore said. "It's your show then."

Dian stood up. "Then unpack your party clothes and I'll see what I can do."

Bel straightened his immaculate black coat, making sure the fold of the wrap style fell correctly against the matching black trousers. He knew better than to wear any hint of color or pattern. Everything about it shouted Calpurnian gentleman, down to his raw silk shirt dyed to exactly the same shade. His hair was freshly cut and pomaded. He looked in the mirror and saw a man of substance, a man who might belong in the rarefied strata to which he aspired.

It was morning. He'd sent his bonafides to one of Antisia's assistants the previous day, and worked his way through the resulting comm call at the Shrine with Sura to coach him. It hadn't been necessary. The documents spoke for themselves, and he was perfectly at home in the persona of a Calpurnian patrician. Yes, Bel thought, with a smile for the man in the mirror, he looked good if he did say so himself. Now it was showtime. If he didn't come off as the Autarch's son at this point, he'd simply be shown to the very elaborate door of the Viceregal Palace. Bel looked at the mirror in its ornately carved frame over a matching table, pale wood an accent against the dark red wall. Very fancy, but the style was Lonoi. He'd bet a bunch of this furniture was original, when it was just the Palace and there was no Calpurnian Viceroy.

A very stern looking man emerged from the chamber beyond. "The Altissima will see you now."

"Thank you," Bel said. He entered, pacing down the wooden floor with its contrasting planks set into an intricate pattern toward the desk at the other end.

The Altissima was perhaps five years his senior, reddish hair cut at her chin, though to his surprise she did not wear a uniform. Instead, she wore a bronze-colored double-breasted coat over trousers of the same color, the natural slub of the silk its only ornament. Her face was thin, a few freckles across her cheekbones. Her green eyes were the pale color of peridots and she wore no makeup. She watched him measuringly as he approached.

Bel stopped a few feet from the desk, making a proper and deep bow. "Altissima Antisia, it is a very great honor."

He looked up to see her frowning. "Turn around," she said. "And walk back toward the doors."

"If you desire," Bel said. This might be the shortest interview in history.

"Now come back."

He complied.

Her expression was appraising. "It might be," she said. "You have something of him about you." Antisia stood. "I served under the Autarch for fifteen years. He was more a father to me than my own. He was an exceptional commander and an exceptional human being, the greatest man I have ever known. For you to claim to be his son…" She broke off.

"I mean no disrespect," Bel said carefully. "I had no idea of any of this until I found these documents among my late mother's papers. But then I suppose she was not my mother, though I had always thought so. I presume my birth mother sent me to foster for my safety." He met her eyes guilelessly. "I have heard of the Altissimus Iulus all my life. I had no idea that I had any connection to someone so rightfully revered and admired."

Antisia looked away. "He would have brought us together if he had not been murdered by people not fit to wash his clothes. Now his assassins are dead in their turn, run to ground by the Hounds of Justice." She looked back at him, sharp green eyes reminding him suddenly of a hunting cat. "One may hide from human justice but not from the vengeance of the gods. Are you afraid of the gods' vengeance?"

"I am not a religious man, Altissima," Bel said with a little bow. Most Calpurnians were not. Just his luck to find one who was.

"Ah." She raised her chin. "What do you fear, then?"

Bel felt considerably on the wrong foot. "I suppose the things that all men fear," he said. "Loss, want…dishonor." The latter was something of a stroke of brilliance. "If I do prove to be the Autarch's son, I will have a great deal to live up to, and I will fear failing at the attempt."

She nodded. "Indeed you will. And you are not certain that you are his son?"

Bel spread his hands. "Altissima, I knew nothing of this until my mother's death, and I have no more evidence than what I have given you. It was her wish that I read these documents and act upon them, but I have no more idea than you whether they are genuine. I hope that they are, for what fatherless boy does not dream that his father is a great hero? But I do not know."

Her eyes did not leave his face. "And you did so?"

Bel looked up at the ceiling, lamps hanging from crossbeams of fragrant wood. "Of course. I imagined who my father might be. I hoped that he was wonderful. I feared that he was not. I pretended that he might suddenly show up and claim me, but of course that was no more than a child's dream. To find these documents… Altissima, I am at a loss. I did not know who he might be until he was dead. More than anything I wish that I had known this a year ago."

"And then he could have told us himself if you were who you claim to be," Antisia said. She took a deep breath. "But your blood will tell its own story. I presume you are willing to undergo a genetic test? A simple blood sample will suffice."

Bel nodded. "Of course. I'd be happy to provide a blood sample."

"Excellent. I will schedule that as soon as possible." Antisia looked at the screen on her desk. "Where are you staying?"

"At one of the hostelries in town," Bel said. There was the in, time to come up with a reason to stay at the Viceregal Palace. "If it would be more convenient, I could stay here in guest quarters."

She frowned. "It wouldn't be appropriate for you to stay here until we have more certainty. However, I trust you will be willing to meet some of Altissimus Iulus' acquaintances?"

"Of course," Bel said courteously. A skeptical woman. He was going to have to be cooperative and flattering. But at least a function in the Viceregal Palace would mean that he was inside and not watched constantly as he was at a solo meeting. "I would be incredibly honored."

"There is a reception this evening," Antisia said. "If you will find it in you to attend at the nineteenth hour?"

"I would be delighted," Bel said with another bow.

"I will arrange for you to go directly to a blood draw," Antisia said. Her eyes were sharp on his face. "I presume you would like certainty as much as I would. These claims you make are quite substantial."

"What I desire most is the truth," Bel said.

"Then we will endeavor to find it as soon as possible," she replied. "And I will see you this evening." She touched the comm on her desk. "Felis, please take this gentleman to the clinic. He is to have a blood draw for genetic sequencing."

"I appreciate your tolerance, Altissima," Bel said sincerely. "I will arrive at the nineteenth hour and place myself at your disposal." At least a reception, unlike a seated dinner, would allow him to move around and perhaps find out where the Solaste Crown was displayed. Surely it would be natural to want to see famous artifacts!

"Until then," the Altissma said, a dismissal if he'd ever heard one.

The door at the far end opened, the same man returning, presumably to escort him to the clinic. "Altissima," Bel said with another bow, and followed him out.

THE CLINIC WAS UTILITARIAN, the blood draw no different than one might expect, a sample taken from his arm by a brisk medic who had no idea what it was for. It took only a few minutes. Presumably the Altissima would have it sent by dispatch boat to Calpurnia in good time. She didn't seem like the sort to dally. Just his luck to find the sort of subordinate who had personally known the man whose son he was claiming to be.

For a moment Bel felt a pang of guilt. She'd be upset when she discovered she'd been taken. Well, not if he professed ignorance himself. He might manage to make it appear that it was an honest mistake. But not if he stole the Solaste Crown. And that was the job. He was here to do a job. That was the whole point. Steal the crown. Steal whatever else was possible and get out. He wouldn't be here when Altissima Antisia found out she'd been lied to. There was no reason whatsoever to imagine her response. He'd be on a merchanter flirting with its pretty captain on his way to Menaechmi when the results of the genetic test came back.

The first thing had been to get the Altissima to accept his claim. The second thing was to locate the crown. That was the task for tonight. He'd make nice at a reception, eat little snacks, and see if he could find out where the antiques were kept. No going for it tonight. He'd just get a general idea and see what the plan was going to have to be.

So it was with a serious and respectable mien that Bel showed up at the Viceregal Palace at 19:00 on the dot. Which meant of course that he was early. All other guests were fashionably late. He knew very well that 19:00 really meant that people would arrive an hour later, but it seemed to Bel that precisely following instructions might express seriousness to Altissima Antisia. She came in ten minutes later as Bel examined the elaborate buffet table without sampling.

"You're here," she said.

"Indeed." Bel inclined his head. "Did you think I'd leave?"

"It occurred to me." Antisia looked at him thoughtfully.

Time for sincerity. "I want to know the truth," Bel said. "It seems this is the only way to find it."

She took a deep breath. "You're no coward at any rate."

"I'd like to think not," Bel said. Certainly running a game like this took balls. What would be his question if he were Nereus? "Altissima, if it is not too painful, what was the Altissimus Iulus like?"

A muscle twitched in her face and then stilled. "Very clever," she said. "Measured. Always thinking. He had a plan and a backup plan and a backup to the backup plan. He danced circles around the Senate. There was always a move inside another move. But it wasn't cruel. Expedient, perhaps. But not cruel." She shook her head. "You must understand, his life was not his own. He could not afford to do things simply because he wanted to. He was not some self-indulgent merchant prince. He was disciplined. And if that meant giving up his son, then so be it."

"I don't think I could live like that," Bel said quietly.

"Probably not." Antisia's voice was sharp. "You are half Lonoi, and they are a passionate people. Calpurnians do not indulge in passion." He couldn't quite make out whether her tone was critical of his supposed flaws or of the sentiment itself. "We step on the Path of Honors when we are small children. We attend the correct primary school where we are weeded by intelligence and conventionality. You do not step on after you are four years old. But you step off. Any flaw, any point at which you do not attend the right lessons or acquire the correct experiences, and you are not bound for the top ranks. By the time you are twenty, you have either achieved or failed."

"And you became Altissimus Iulus' aide?"

"Obviously I had achieved." Antisia snapped her fingers and a waiter appeared, a tumbler of liquor with ice in it on a tray, which he presented to Antisia with a bow. She took a substantial drink. "Tell him what you want and he'll fetch it."

"Wine, please," Bel asked. Starting with hard liquor this early would mean that his head wasn't as clear as it needed to be.

Antisia seemed to have no such compunction. She drained the glass and put it back on the tray. "Bring me another," she directed.

Guests began to arrive. It seemed to Bel that he stood there forever being introduced to one after another. All of them were dressed alike, which did make it hard to remember who they were. All of them wore sharply tailored black suits as he and Antisia did, though hers was more severely cut than most. Remember them by pieces of jewelry? That was a memnomic. The woman with the butterfly pin. The man with the diamond bracelet. The man with the matching ruby rings on each hand. Otherwise it was a sea of black-dressed people not enjoying themselves at all while wondering who would be the first to breach the buffet table.

Bel bowed to another elderly couple and straightened up just as the assistant announced the next arrivals. "The Ladies Melian, of House Melian on Menaechmi."

She wore gray, a suit as sharply cut as any of the men here, the shoulders padded and the front open enough to see an immaculate white shirt with white-on-white embroidery. Her unruly hair was sleek, her face defined by heavy makeup, but it was unmistakably Aurore, the merchant captain. Heads turned. The other woman was even more startling. Her black trousers and white shirt were topped with a long coat in a rich blue color, thick with golden embroidery. Her hair was longer and worn down, lighter than Aurore's, the tips of it dipped in blue that matched her coat, framing her angular, haughty face.

They made their way toward the receiving line. Could he bolt? Not without being extremely obvious. He was standing next to the Altissima. Leaving in a hurry would raise questions. And now an old gentleman was asking him something and he had to reply. By the time Bel looked up they were coming down the line.

He knew the exact moment Aurore saw him. Her eyes widened just slightly between lengthened lashes. Bel gave her what he hoped was a conspiratorial glance. Why oh why hadn't it occurred to him that the captain might also be the owner? Well, because it was a Menaechman merchant house. Surely house members ought to be lounging on a beach somewhere, not climbing around the hull in the rain! What kind of merchant princess did her own refits?

Aurore frowned. He waggled an eyebrow, which he hoped conveyed that they could talk privately later if she just didn't blow his cover the moment she reached him in the receiving line. The Altissima was right next to him.

Then she was in front of him. "May I present the possible Nereus Iulus?" the Altissima said, as she'd said fifty times already.

"Aurore Melian," Aurore said. Her frown deepened.

"I am honored," Bel said with a little bow. "I have heard a great deal of you and your starships. Perhaps we could discuss them as the evening progresses?"

Her disapproving expression should have curdled milk. "Yes, I think that would be agreeable," Aurore said. "I am eager to talk about our starships." There was definitely an edge in her voice. Ok, she wouldn't call him on it now, but he'd better catch her as soon as he could and come up with a good reason why he had two different names.

"I shall look forward to it with great pleasure," Bel said.

The line moved. "Dian Melian," the other woman said. She was looking past him at the Altissima.

"A pleasure," Bel said.

She moved before he had a chance to say anything else. "Dian Melian, Altissima. It is indeed a pleasure to meet our renowned host."

"I'm hardly renowned as a host," the Altissima said dryly.

"Did I say so?" Dian's brows rose. "And yet you have distinction, if not…" she gestured around the party, "for sparkling gatherings. Still, we must all do what we must do."

"Indeed." The Altissima seemed to be actually seeing her, a first for the evening. "And is it your custom, Lady Melian, to wear plebian clothing to a formal affair?" Amid the sea of black suits, Dian Melian's blue and gold coat stood out like some exotic bird amid a gathering of crows.

"Am I plebian?" Dian asked innocently. "I thought I was just signaling that lovers could aspire."

For a second the Altissima looked like she'd choke. Then she actually smiled. "If that is your intention, Lady Melian, you convey it most clearly." A little bow, and the line moved on.

Aurore glanced back at him at the end. He was going to have to get away soon.

CHAPTER
THREE

ALTISSIMA ANTISIA GESTURED to the waiter who took her empty glass and supplied her with a filled one. The receiving line was over. She had dealt with the stuffiest of transient aristocracy, most of them elderly and all of them timid. She'd assured everyone that of course Lono was a safe place to be, ridiculous as that was. Any moment Thurinia would lay claim to it and she had the ships to back it up. Best intelligence suggested that nine to eleven ships of the line had escaped Morrigan and rallied to her cause, either before Cassian had been killed or after. In Antisia's opinion, next to Cassian she was the worst of the lot, as bad as Altissima Gnea had been. Her smug virtue grated at every turn. And yet she was probably going to be Autarch. She'd take Calpurnia in the worst possible direction, Social Logic. But what was the alternative?

Antisia took a long slug of her drink. Fight her with six ships and four of them not even spaceworthy? She recoiled at the thought. She hadn't even been aboard *Cornelia* since they'd arrived at Lono. If it were up to her, she'd never set foot on a warship again. She looked around the room, full of boring, petty people doing boring, petty socializing, just as they did all the time, everyone in their proper social position, talking about the same things year after year. And yet they were hers. They were her responsibility. She could imagine vividly a missile slamming home, the flash and the shockwave knocking down walls, tearing arms from torsos, old ladies in black lying with their trousers and legs torn off…

"I'm glad to catch you alone for a moment, Altissima," a sultry voice said beside her.

Antisia blinked. The scene she imagined had been so real. It took a moment to realize it wasn't. The reception room was intact. Dian Melian was standing beside her, a glass of wine in her hand. "Lady Melian."

Those dark eyes were studying her. "I appreciate the invitation to your reception."

"It is nothing," Antisia said with an abbreviated bow.

She glanced around the room calculatingly, then back to Antisia. "True. But I suppose I must get used to it since I will be here for months."

"Months?" Antisia said. "I thought you and your sister were simply refitting a merchant ship at Tranquility Yards."

"You are miraculously well-informed," Dian said. "However, we are unable to leave until *Golden Wanderer*'s refit is complete. Which may take months, I am told." She lifted her wineglass to her lips. "We have paid for six missiles which cannot be delivered by the fitter because you have requisitioned them all. So I have no missiles, and you have all of them."

Ah. That was the problem. "Regretfully," Antisia said, "I must reserve all available ordnance. You understand."

"I do not," Dian said. "Surely you have plenty and I only need six. For which I have already paid. So I must wait until they are available. Even if that means being trapped in these dreary parties for months." She gave Antisia a sideways smile. "You will not be rid of me as long as you have my missiles."

"Then what incentive is that to supply them?" Antisia asked. There was something about those dark eyes as heady as the distilled liquor over ice. One could actually engage in repartee.

Dian leaned a little closer. "I do like a lady with a missile."

"And what kind of missiles do you like?"

"Electric ones, surely." Dian smirked. "With lots of settings."

Antisia feared that she gulped. "I see," she managed.

"But perhaps I've misunderstood," Dian said. Her voice was practically a purr. She wore a heavy gold collar just inside the neckline of her white shirt. "If you don't have any missiles..."

"I do," Antisia said. It was hard to keep her eyes off that collar, six-sided links like a honeycomb. Or off those thin, ironic lips. This was the point in the evening when drink soothed all to a muddy whirl anyway. "But I can't give them to you."

Dian bent close enough that her blue-tipped hair brushed against Antisia's shoulder. "You could show me your missiles, surely?"

"Much as I would like to," Antisia said, "the party..."

"...is boring and pointless and like every other you've been to," Dian said. "Except that I'm here. So why not take advantage of your privilege to have a little fun? Surely someone like me doesn't drop in every day?"

"Never," Antisia said. She felt she ought to make something clear. "I'm only interested in women."

"I would never have guessed," Dian said innocently, and then her eyes cut back with a knowing look. "I prefer women myself. With missiles."

"Are we talking about toys or ordnance?"

"Both." Dian laughed. She was standing too close.

"I can't give you any ordnance." Antisia thought she should make that clear, though it felt like saying *try harder*. Well, it was certainly wrong to bend rules for sexual favors, but really at this point what did it matter? They'd continue this endless reception until Thurinia called in the chips and everybody died. Or at least she died and Thurinia took Lono. Same difference. She met Dian's eyes. "You and your sister should leave," she said quietly. "Get out of here before something terrible happens."

Dian inclined her head, then looked up. Her eyes were startlingly honest. "I can't do that," she said. "I have a duty too."

"Which involves sleeping with me to get the missiles?"

"No sleeping will be involved," Dian said. That wicked smirk was back. "I didn't agree to perversion."

"Beg pardon?"

Dian extended a hand with the wineglass in it. "Look, you know it's not dutiful and virtuous to sex a degenerate foreigner who's throwing herself at you for favors. But why not? What's the point of being Altissima if it's nothing but a shit-show? Surely if you're going down, you could have a little fun first."

"You might be my last chance?" The world seemed a little fuzzy from alcohol, but that wasn't all of it. She hadn't said these things. Was her mood so obvious? Or her situation?

"Or not." There was that expression again. "You roll the dice. Sometimes it's dogs and sometimes it's the lady."

"Why not?" Antisia said. She'd been careful all her life. She'd cultivated her reputation and perfected her record. And what was it good for at the end? "I have a suite upstairs." She smiled. "With a collection of missiles."

"Perfect." Dian touched her arm lightly. "Let me tell my sister where I'm going so she doesn't worry."

Aurore looked around the reception room, trying to appear bored instead of stressed. No one was talking to her. Which was how it usually worked at parties, unless it was the kind of party where everyone wanted to bend the ear of House Melian's heir. She was still nursing her first glass of wine and trying to look world-weary. Dian had cornered the Altissima and seemed to be pouring on the charm. Well, that was the reason they were here. It certainly wasn't for fun.

It wasn't that Aurore didn't like parties. She liked them well enough with a few close friends. Unlike everyone else in her House who seemed to thrive on chaos, Aurore preferred quiet times spent with people she knew deeply. Dinner with two people she'd been close to for years was infinitely preferable to a big, noisy party. She had true friends. She knew who she could count on. The constant social whirl of House Melian gave her a headache.

But she could do it. She'd been trained to it from childhood. She was her father's heir, heir to House Melian and everything that entailed, and she knew exactly what was expected of her and who counted on her for what. It was an enviable position; half the people in Beira would kill to be her. If only she wanted to be her.

Aurore picked up her full glass and attempted to look occupied. She was no good at small talk. What was she supposed to do with herself while Dian sweet-talked the Altissima? And there, on the other side of the reception room, was Bel Alan or whatever his name was. He was slipping out a door. People on honest business, or people looking for the sanitary facilities, didn't slip out. They walked out. The only people who slipped out were up to no good. Aurore put her glass down on the nearest column base and made her way through the crowd, striding out the door not far behind him.

The long gallery beyond seemed empty at first. The lights were low, illuminating only the portraits or artifacts displayed along the walls, the wooden statue of a seabird sitting on its nest in the middle of the hall. This was official space, but not in use tonight.

Bel was at the far end examining a display case. Then he frowned, turning to look for something.

"Not looking for me?" Aurore said, striding down the gallery.

For a moment he looked distracted, before he greeted her with a charming smile. "Aurore! What a pleasure it is to see you tonight!"

She stopped with a meter between them. "Is it a pleasure, Bel Alan? Or is it Nereus Iulus?"

He winced. "Discretion, dear lady. Please lower your voice."

"I am not your dear lady. And I'm very curious as to which you are. Or are both of them aliases?" She looked around the gallery. "There are a lot of valuable things in here, aren't there?"

"It's complicated," he said.

"Then let's start with the basics," Aurore said. "Your name?"

He sighed. "My name is Bel Alan."

"Then why were you just introduced as Nereus Iulus, possible son of the Autarch?" Aurore put her hands on her hips. "I have no intention of being the escape plan for some kind of criminal scheme. I am not a criminal and I will certainly not involve House Melian in something illegal that will impact our ability to do business on Lono."

"You didn't say you were the heir to the House, did you?" Bel retorted. "You implied you were just the captain."

"I did not lie," Aurore said. "I told you my name. You concluded I was nobody important based on my clothing. That's your own prejudices, not deception on my part." Lots of people had made that mistake. It was nice to finally call someone on it.

"I didn't think you were nobody important. I thought you were the ship's captain."

"I am the ship's captain. And I am the owner's daughter. Those things are not contradictory," Aurore said.

Bel held his hands up. "No, no, they're not. Fine. It's all good. You're the ship's captain. And the Melian of Melian."

"But who are you?" Aurore said insistently. "Because I would really like to hear a good reason not to go out there and tell everyone that you're Bel Alan." She took a step back, keeping well out of easy reach. "If you're some kind of thief casing the joint…"

He took a deep breath. "Will you keep your voice down? I'm Lonoi Resistance."

"You're what?"

"Lonoi Resistance," Bel said quietly. "Look, you know Lono is an occupied world. We were conquered by Calpurnia eighty years ago. Half of Tranquility was burned. Tens of thousands of people were killed or rounded up and taken off-world. Since then there's always been a Resistance. There have always been people who wanted to liberate their world." He took a step toward her. "Right now, Calpurnia is weak. We've got a chance at making some progress."

He looked sincere. Aurore considered his face. How would she know? She wished she had her father's gift for reading people and seeing through their masks. But it made sense. It made sense that there was a Lonoi Resistance and that now would be the time for them to move. Calpurnia was at best in chaos, at worst in decline after the loss of so many ships at Morrigan. And why not? Why wouldn't Lono want to be free? Her father had worked to keep Menaechmi out of Calpurnian hands. They were arming their merchant ships against Calpurnia, and probably one of these days she'd get the battle she craved. If there was a Lonoi Resistance, they were friends, or should be.

Aurore nodded slowly. "I see," she said. "So you're pretending to be Nereus Iulus? Why?"

"To find a thing called the Solaste Crown," Bel said. "It was the emblem of the old monarchy. It's an emblem of Lonoi sovereignty. It's somewhere in this palace. I'm supposed to return it to the Resistance."

"And then?"

He smiled self-deprecatingly. "Then I'll be the most wanted man on the planet. So I was arranging passage off-world as an alternative to capture and execution. Which is where you came in."

That actually made sense. "Ok," Aurore said. "Do you know where this thing is?"

"Not yet," Bel said. "And I've got a limited amount of time to find it. When they get the results of the genetic test back from Calpurnia and realize I'm not the Autarch's heir, at the very least they'll dump me out if I haven't got the Crown by then. So I need to find it and disappear before the test comes back." He looked at her. "If I still have passage to Menaechmi?"

Aurore nodded slowly. "You do. But I can't raise ship yet. We haven't loaded our ordnance."

"I don't have the crown yet either."

"Yes, but I don't know when we will have it," she said. "The Altissima is sitting on all the ordnance."

"And you can't leave without it to save a man's life?" Bel implored.

Aurore sighed. "I suppose if it comes to that," she said. "My father will have a fit, but if we can't get the missiles, we can't get them. And you don't have this crown anyway yet."

"Not yet," Bel said. "I slipped off from the party to see if it was displayed in one of the public galleries, but no such luck."

"Why would it be?" Aurore asked.

Bel gestured to the cases along the wall, heavy plasticine like that used for habitat domes. Beneath the transparent surface was a display of jewelry and little carved animals and a mask inlaid with hundreds of tiny pieces of seashell. Each had a neat little screen beside it, scrolling text describing the object. "Anthropological artifacts," he said. "Our culture on display."

"And that's offensive?" Aurore asked quietly. "Are these objects that are private?"

Bel huffed. "No. They're ordinary, most of them. It's not people seeing them that's the problem. It's the tone. Quaint and primitive things belonging to someone else, not our own things with a history displayed so that people will understand them better. As though our culture was a commodity to be traded."

"My culture is a commodity," Aurore said. "We're happy to sell you anything you like. You want our coffee or our silks or our entertainment? We expect currency upfront. That's soft power. Calpurnia buys our culture, and we're the canker in their rose. We're the whisper under the surface—you don't have to live like this. You could come away." She dropped her voice on the last phrase, low and seductive.

Bel looked startled. "That's a different way of looking at it."

"If people want your culture, they give you a measure of control over theirs."

"Your whole planet tops from the bottom," Bel said.

Aurore laughed. "If you like. My father would probably agree with that assessment completely."

"That's something I'll think about," Bel said seriously. "But what I need to do now is find the Solaste Crown."

"Maybe there's another gallery?" Aurore asked. "If it's not in this one."

The door at the far end leading to the reception opened. Bel clasped her hands, drawing her closer and looking at her plaintively over their hands. "Oh Aurore," he said.

"Well, I'm glad you're enjoying the party," Dian said.

Aurore dropped his hands like they were radioactive. "Dian. It's not…"

"I don't really care," Dian said. "I'm not your chaperone. I was sticking my head in to tell you that I'll find my own way home tonight."

"You…what?" Aurore was flustered. She'd missed a beat. And to think that she and Bel… Well, she wouldn't!

Dian was looking at her like she expected Aurore to get some message. "I said, I'll find my own way back to the ship later. Don't worry."

The Altissima. Right. Dian had moved that fast? What in the name of the Infernal was it with her family? "Dad-levels of charm?" Aurore asked.

Dian smirked. "You got it."

There was certainly no denying that her father would sex the Altissima if it would get the missiles. If Altissimus Cassian had demanded sexual favors instead of currency, he might be alive now. Still, this might not be a good idea when it came down to it. "Dian, are you sure?"

"Absolutely. See you later." Dian waved in her direction. "Just keep on doing…whatever it is you're doing. Lovely to see you, Nereus Iulus." She exited stage center.

Aurore sat down on one of the carved column bases.

"You ok?" Bel asked.

Aurore nodded. "Yes. I'm not her chaperone either. It's just that my sister can be a little…emotionally fragile."

Bel looked after Dian. "Do you need to go after her?"

"She wouldn't thank me." After all, that was the plan. Though perhaps naïvely Aurore had thought it would go no further than sweet-talking. She took a deep breath. "Dian is twenty-four. It's not on me."

Bel shrugged. "So how about helping me look for the Crown? If anyone sees me wandering around the galleries alone, it's suspicious. If I'm wandering around with a lovely lady…"

"…it's courtship," Aurore finished.

Bel's eyebrow rose. "Courtship?"

"I told you, I have serious relationships with serious men. I don't do pick-ups."

He smiled. "Courtship, then. Surely Nereus Iulus can court a merchant princess?"

"That makes a fine cover story," Aurore said. She took his arm. "So let's return to the party for a little while and be seen, and then explore some of these other rooms. The Solaste Crown has to be here somewhere."

. . .

Antisia lay back on the pillow, her head spinning. She heard Dian shift, putting the toys on the side table. She opened her eyes.

Dian stretched against the sheets, gloriously naked except for her honeycomb collar and either completely confident in her beauty or simply indifferent. She had a satisfied little smirk. "So," she said, "do you have a personal name, or shall I stick at Altissima?"

It was awkward but unavoidable. "Victoria," she said. "But I don't think anyone calls me that." Not anyone alive, she refrained from saying.

"Antisia then, if you prefer it." Dian reached down and pulled the covers over them both. "Chilly in here."

"The entire palace is drafty," Antisia said.

"You are in fact the person who could do something about that," Dian pointed out.

"It's not my palace."

Dian looked at her critically. "Starting to sober up?"

"Unfortunately." Those too-knowing dark eyes rested like a weight on her. But it had been a fair bargain, hadn't it? She should never have done this, but having done it there was at least the honor of her obligations. "I suppose I might be able to find a few missiles for you."

Lengthened eyelashes swept shut. "Pity," she said lightly. "If it took longer, I might have to see you again."

As though that were something one might want to do? "I don't have them today," Antisia said cautiously.

The smirk grew. "Well, perhaps we could go somewhere."

"There isn't anywhere to go," Antisia said. The covers were chilly. Dian was warm, but she didn't move to embrace her. That would be unbearably intimate, much more so than drunk sex.

Dian looked at her. "There is an entire planet," she said flatly. "Bars, restaurants, clubs, gambling dens, theaters… It cannot be true that there is nowhere to go." She turned on her side, propped on her arm on the pillow. "So either you don't go anywhere, or you'd rather not go with me."

Antisia blinked at her. "Are you always woundingly honest?"

"No. Sometimes I'm a very good liar." And there were those dark eyes again, measuring her.

"I'll get you the missiles and you should leave," Antisia said quietly.

"Before Thurinia gets here?" Dian's voice was as low.

Antisia nodded. "There's no reason for you and your sister to be mixed up in this."

"You could leave."

Antisia smiled mirthlessly. "And go where? In what? My crews stayed loyal to Altissimus Iulus. At the least they'll be imprisoned or reeducated and at worst they'll be executed. And then there are the people here, citizens who don't deserve to die over who's Autarch. I've gambled and lost. But I won't desert the people who trust me and run away."

Her brows twitched. Her flawless makeup was a perfect mask, but her eyes were calculating. "Well," Dian said. "How many ships does Thurinia have? It can't be more than twelve, or maybe fifteen at the outside."

"I am not about to start giving you troop numbers," Antisia said. "I'm not quite that much of an idiot."

"What, because we connived at the destruction of a Calpurnian frigate?" Dian said innocently. "Surely the assassin Cassian was no friend of yours. He came to Beira, demanded reinforcements, kidnapped my baby brother, and nearly killed my father. What would you expect us to do? Besides, you're rid of him."

"The enemy of my enemy is my friend?" Antisia asked.

"Let's just say the enemy of your enemy is not your enemy," Dian said.

"I'll allow that," Antisia said. She lifted one soft, blue-tipped strand of hair. Lovely, fascinating, with something brittle just under the surface. "I've never been to Menaechmi," she said with something like regret in her voice. Now she'd never go.

"You mean you've never shaken us down?" Dian turned over, bare breasts provocatively displayed.

"Not personally."

She smirked. "Here's the thing about Menaechmi. We spread our legs for whoever puts a warship in orbit. To a point."

"Should I take that as a warning about Menaechmi or about you?" Antisia asked.

The smirk grew broader. "Both. I am all Menaechmi."

"I don't expect to find out," Antisia said.

Dian reached up, stroking her hair and pulling her down beside her. "You really are in a corner, aren't you?" Antisia nodded. She didn't truly trust her voice, not with a kind touch. "What about this Nereus Iulus? Is he a card on the table?"

"Maybe. Probably not." Antisia rested her cheek against Dian's shoulder, skin so smooth and soft.

"Is he actually the Autarch's son?"

"He could be. I don't know." Dian's hand kept stroking her hair. "The Autarch told me years ago that Nereus existed and that he hadn't seen him since he was a few months old." Antisia closed her eyes. She'd been honored by the confidence, standing together on the balcony of his office where no one could overhear, the closest thing to a daughter Iulus had. "It was too dangerous. His mother had royal blood. A child who was his and Lonoi royalty could claim both heritages—could claim Lono. This was soon after he'd been made Viceroy of Lono. If Adelphi is the jewel of Calpurnian provinces, Lono is the beating heart. We need the mineral wealth and we need the starship yards. Since we took Lono, we've moved a lot of our heavy industry here. It's allowed us to clean up our pollution problems. The skies of Calpurnia are clear again." Skies she would never see again.

"It's very convenient for him to appear now," Dian said. "He could be an opportunist."

"Well, I'll know when the genetic test comes back," Antisia said. "But if he is indeed the Autarch's heir, I'm afraid he's just as screwed as I am. He'd do better to pretend he'd never heard of it and get out while he can."

"Because Thurinia will kill him?"

Victoria Antisia looked up at her. Even her chin managed to be beautiful. "You're perceptive. Of course she'll kill him. Nothing could be a bigger threat to her than Iulus' natural son."

"Forgive me, but the thing I'm unclear about is this: why don't you just make common cause with Thurinia? Hand over your ships and shake hands? Surely an alliance would make sense to her."

"If I surrender to Thurinia, she'll be Autarch." She closed her eyes again. She was talking too much, but it didn't matter. There was so little time left. "Six more ships and all their crews. She'll sweep the board. But if I fight her, I'll take out some of hers."

"And she'll destroy some of yours," Dian said. "So even if she wins, she won't have nearly as complete a victory as she would have. And maybe you'll kill her."

"It's possible." She could imagine it easily, the other ships providing covering fire for the real move, *Cornelia* on a ceaseless course for Thurinia's flagship, to ram and take them both out. With all significant faction leaders dead, the Senate would have to step up. They'd have to actually govern again. A lovely idea, but even the thought of setting foot in *Cornelia*'s command center made her hands shake. In the end, the weakness was hers.

"And she will kill you," Dian said flatly. "Well, I don't like that."

Antisia raised her head. That had sounded so incongruously petulant, childish defiance of the fates. "You don't like it?"

"I don't like it," Dian said. "So I will have to think of another alternative."

"Oh." Antisia didn't laugh. That would be rude. "Well, you just do that then."

"I shall," Dian said imperiously. "Provided you take me out and show me a good time."

"If I take you out and show you a good time, you'll save my life?" Antisia said bemusedly.

"I think that's fair, don't you?" She smiled, one hand curling around Antisia's shoulder.

"Absolutely," Antisia said. Why not spend some time in her last days enjoying herself? It would give her something to think about besides anticipating those last seconds on *Cornelia*. "So a restaurant then? I'll see if I can locate something suitable. Do you prefer stuffy and formal or less so?"

"Less stuffy. But not a bar." She glanced away. "I'd rather not drink too much."

And it would probably be best to stay marginally sober the entire evening, Antisia thought. "A less stuffy restaurant. Shall I ping you with the reservation?"

"That would be ideal." Dian sat up, the curve of her back surely one of the wonders of nature. "But I should get back to the ship."

"I'll take you," Antisia said. To pack her off in a trundle would be to treat her like a streetwalker. She would at least escort her to the dockyard rather than stay in her chilly bed.

"If you like," Dian said with a little smile as she hunted for her underwear.

CHAPTER
FOUR

BEL TOOK public transportation to the Shrine, arriving with ten or so morning worshippers and pilgrims. Several of them had guidebooks on their handhelds and were chatting excitedly. Calpurnians, Bel thought, who wanted to broaden their experience of the universe. He blended in with them nicely. After all, he was completely in favor of broadening his experience of the universe. Menaechmi sounded like a great place for a long vacation. Presuming he could manage to get the Solaste Crown and some incidentals.

The young acolyte had come out and was talking to the huddle of tourists and pilgrims. Her eyes widened a little bit when she saw him, and Bel gave her a friendly smile, holding up his downloaded guidebook. "We are delighted to welcome you to the Shrine of the Lord of the Dance," she said. "We hope that you will find your visit enlightening. I will request that you do not take images inside the Shrine itself. Also, if you need sanitary facilities, please let me know and I will direct you. There will also be no consumption of food or beverages inside the Shrine. Please do not touch the Image or any paintings on the walls. They are fragile and can be damaged by the oil on your fingers." She smiled to make her words less unfriendly. "Let us begin by taking our shoes off at the door. Please bring them with you so that you will have them when we go on the terrace."

Bel trailed the crowd going in. He suspected Sura would know very quickly that he was in the group. It would be easy to slip off for a private conversation. He took off his shoes in the vestibule, looking around like any tourist who'd never been here before. And he'd only been here once, hadn't he? There was no reason for it to feel so familiar.

There was a doorway covered by a long hanging curtain, scarlet with a faint design on it. Behind it was a hallway that led to the private rooms of the acolytes and… And something. There was a reason he shouldn't go there. Bel put his hand on the doorway, drawing aside the curtain. There was the hallway lit by one indirect light, four plain doors off it.

…he stood in front of one of the doors. It was open, stairs leading down. They seemed enormous, gigantic, unreal. They led down to a corner, a curve, a faint blue light. "Bel!" someone said, catching him around the waist. "You can't go that way." An acolyte, her black robe contrasting with her pretty young face.

"Why?" he asked.

"There are monsters sleeping down there," she whispered. "Sleeping in the dark…"

"Bel?" The tour had moved on. Sura stood behind him. "I'm glad you've come to speak with me."

"Yes. Yes, of course." Bel frowned, letting the curtain drop. He turned. He was almost a head taller than Sura, if one didn't count her headdress of white braids.

Her eyes rested on him. "Is something troubling you?"

"What's down there?" he asked abruptly.

Her eyebrows rose. "The kitchen," she said. "Storerooms."

"Not the acolytes' rooms?" He couldn't bring himself to ask about the stairs.

"No, they're in the other wing." Sura's voice was even, but there was something not right in it. "Why?"

"I just wondered."

"Let us go into my office where we will not be disturbed by the tour," Sura said.

"Of course." He followed her through the main room of the Shrine, stopping behind her as she made a deep bow to the Image. Its eyes followed him.

There was a second chair in her office and he sat as she sank down onto the kneeling chair. "I presume you had questions or difficulties?" Sura asked.

Bel nodded. "I'm in, and the Altissima doesn't disbelieve me. She's taken a blood sample for DNA sequencing, but she's not letting me lodge in the Viceregal Palace yet. I did get a chance to look around last night. I didn't find the crown. It's not in the public galleries. I was wondering if you might have any theories about where it might be. Or at least anything that might be useful for me to know." He leaned forward. "Tell me about the Solaste Crown. Where did it come from? What's its history, other than the last Prince had it?"

"As I believe I told you before, it was a gift to the Princess Lutece Calado from the Warlord of Morrigan some eight hundred years ago." She smiled. "His name was Khreesos, and when he came to Lono we had not had contact with any other world since the first settlement. He came offering us technology and trade and knowledge of worlds we had not even dreamed existed. We had sailing ships and water-looms. He had starships. While there were many of us that were frightened, Princess Lutece saw an opportunity. Or at least she saw the man. Our ballads say that they were greatly taken with one another, recognizing in one another peerless warriors and devoted leaders."

Bel smiled. "Don't ballads always say things like that?"

"I imagine so," Sura said. "But whatever their reasons, they conceived a child together. And yet Khreesos could not stay. His destiny called him, out there beyond the stars. And so he gave the Solaste Crown to Lutece, a gift for their daughter yet unborn, a gift that only she could use and that would secure her throne. And then he went on. He met his destiny and never returned." Her voice dropped, a storyteller's conceit. "Their daughter was born, and in due time she became Princess Nadicce after her mother. It was she who first called the Phoenix of the Sun."

"Beg pardon?" Bel said.

"The Phoenix of the Sun," Sura said. "A strange, legendary beast that would come only to the greatest of the Calado Princes. For some centuries it appeared at their wish, and then the line grew thin and the rulers weak, and it came no more. Only the rightful wearer of the Solaste Crown might command it, or so the story went."

"And when was this monster last seen?" Bel asked. There was a chill along his spine.

"At the coronation of Prince Dercinge, two hundred and thirty-four years ago," Sura said. "He was the last strong ruler. But he was assassinated by his cousin, and the Phoenix has not been seen since then."

"Let me guess," Bel said. "If the Solaste Crown were worn by the rightful heir, it would reappear." That was the kind of thing that happened in stories.

"Indeed," Sura said with a smile. "If the Solaste Crown were claimed by the Blameless Prince or Princess, the Phoenix of the Sun would return and we would be free."

"This is crazy," Bel snapped. "It's just a story."

"Probably." Sura did not argue. "But stories have power. Your concern is to simply acquire the crown. What I do with it after that is none of your affair."

"Good. Yes." Bel rubbed his hands against his pants legs. "I just… I don't want to be part of starting some pointless rebellion that will get a lot of people killed."

Her eyebrows rose. "Why?"

Bel shook his head. "Because people don't have enough as it is. They just want to get to work in the yards and make enough to feed their kids. They want to have a little fun sometimes. They're lucky, because they live here and not on Calpurnia and they can do things their way. And yeah, they've got less currency but they don't live in a tiny little box with every move they make going down on their permanent record. It sounds great to rebel for freedom, but they've already got more freedom than anyone there. I don't want some asshole to get them to start something and get killed. They're worth too much for that." He stood up. "I don't want to be part of that plan."

Sura looked—something. Shocked? But maybe he saw a flash of something else just before her face stilled. "My plan is to return the

Solaste Crown to the Lonoi people," Sura said. "And if the Blameless Prince should ever come, I do not think he would want Lono destroyed in a hopeless gesture. That would not be the action of a worthy prince." She gestured to the chair. "So unless you are refusing to complete the job, please sit down and let us finish."

Slowly, Bel sat back down. Something wasn't right here. The only way to find out the game was to keep playing. "Ok," he said.

Sura took a deep breath. "So if the Solaste Crown is not in the public spaces, it's probably in a safe or a vault somewhere."

"Do you have any idea where?"

She shook her head. "If the Calpurnians have installed a vault, I don't know where it would be. The old treasure room when it was a Lonoi palace has been turned into one of the reception rooms. I presume they'd want a vault to be somewhere private. But beyond that…" She spread her hands.

Bel nodded. "On the ground floor. With an entrance from a room that isn't open to the public. That's hard because it looks like the palace is constructed around a series of courtyards. There aren't a lot of interior areas that don't have windows."

"I'd be surprised if there were any," Sura said. "The old palace dates back before the adoption of electrical light and heat. Every room that was going to be in use needed windows."

"That makes it easier," Bel said. "I need to look for alterations in architecture. Bricked up windows. That kind of thing. Places where modern design clashes with the original design." He stood up. "Thank you. That's helpful."

"If there is anything else I can do, please let me know," Sura said.

SURA WATCHED BEL LEAVE, her hands clasped together inside the bell sleeves of her outer robe. He had a swing in his step, an energetic young man. No, not so young. Thirty. And there were creases at the corners of his eyes showing where lines of strain would be at forty, if he lived so long. A con artist. A gambler. She shook her head.

Her acolyte came to stand beside her. "Should I follow him, Sura?"

Sura shook her head. "No need. We know where he will go."

"What if he simply gets on the starship and leaves?" her acolyte asked.

"He won't do that." Sura's voice was confident. "He is imagining a vault full of glittering things."

Her acolyte drew in a breath hesitantly. "Is this a good idea? This man?"

"He is the man there is," Sura said. "Now return to your duties." She walked out on the terrace. The rain had stopped, a few diffuse wisps of sun cutting through the clouds. The buds on the apple tree were swelling. A few were beginning to show a faint flush of pink. Clouds of steam and fume rose from the factories of Tranquility across the estuary. And down in the darkness, something stirred.

Lord of Hounds and Justice, Sura thought, *if I have done wrong, let the punishment fall on me, not on Bel. He is blameless in this.* She bent her head, her braids as heavy as a crown.

AURORE WAS on her third cup of coffee in *Golden Wanderer*'s common room when Dian emerged from her cabin. Everyone else was enjoying the freedom of the port until midday. "Good morning," she said.

"Ugh," Dian said, going to get her own cup. "I will never get used to a planet with a 26-hour day-night cycle."

Aurore felt it was best to just jump in there. "Dian, when you said charm, I thought you meant talking. I never asked you to sex the Altissima for the missiles."

Dian leaned back on the counter with the cup in her hands. "We said Dad-levels of charm. Don't you think Dad would have sexed the Altissima?"

"Dad is not always the best example," Aurore said.

"Tell me about it." Dian raised the cup and took a quick drink. "Ow, that's hot. But I've got the missiles, or will soon. She promised them and I think she'll deliver. Now is the part where you say, good job, Dian."

"Good job, Dian," Aurore said. "You're brilliant." There was no point in not saying it at this point.

"I know." Dian smiled. "And truly, it was fine. She's interesting in a messed-up way. If you like gloomy and doomed."

"I suppose." Aurore looked at her askance.

Dian took another drink. This time her eyes were serious. "But you never sex anyone, do you? When was the last time you had someone?"

"I don't know." Aurore shrugged. "Everyone who comes on to me has an ulterior motive. They want House Melian's heir, not me. I'm not interested in being used for my money."

"That's why I only keep mistresses," Dian said. "Short contracts, everything aboveboard. Everybody knows exactly what they're getting. It's an honest transaction." She gestured with her cup at Aurore. "Better than wondering what their ulterior motive is."

"I've got this silly idea that someone will fall in love with me," Aurore said. "With me, not House Melian."

"You know the only way out of that, don't you?" Dian took another sip. "Have the guts to tell Dad that you don't want to be House Heir."

"I can't do that," Aurore demurred.

"He does not actually lack children. Even if he's decided I'm too unstable, there's darling baby Theo."

"He's twelve," Aurore said.

"So is Dad planning to kick it soon? He seems to be going strong. He told Genisse that he wasn't sure this baby was the last." She winced at Aurore. "I know! What's he planning to do? Father number six at sixty? Seriously, there's a point where it's too much. Just tell him you don't want to be the Heir. He has options."

Aurore sighed. She couldn't say what she thought: *I hoped that you'd get it together enough that he'd name you, but he's not confident in you. He thinks you're a screw up, and he's not going to leave House Melian to a screw up or a twelve-year-old.* "Maybe," Aurore temporized. "At some point." She shook her head. "But this thing with the Altissima..."

"She said she'd ping me." Dian tossed her head. "Frankly, I doubt it. But she did say she'd release the missiles."

Just like that. She never understood Dian. "Isn't there something you want? Somebody you'd want a relationship with that you weren't paying?"

"They'd have to be completely codependent," Dian said. "And

need me utterly. You know, light of their life, purpose and meaning, all of that."

You mean madly in love with you, Aurore nearly said, but didn't. She understood why Dian considered herself entirely unlovable. "You've seen one too many counselors," she said instead.

"Probably." Dian put the empty cup down on the counter. "Which one of the nineteen was too many? I'm sticking to mistresses now. I'd rather be a wastrel than a fuck-up. It's much more pleasant." She ruffled Aurore's hair as she went past. "But you've got to tell Dad sooner or later if you're not going to do it. It's not going to get easier."

"I know," Aurore said to her retreating back.

She'd known she was heir to House Melian her entire life. The first time she remembered going to the port offices with her father, she must have been quite small. He'd showed her everything, carried her on his shoulder down the flight line to see the merchanters pulled up snug to Melian's berths, four of them, each and every one with the golden honeybee on its prow. They were hers, her father said. They belonged to every member of House Melian, her included. Each person had a share in House ventures. The prosperity of one family member was the prosperity of all.

The Melian captain had stood beneath a ship to talk to her father. She looked up at its curved surface, at the smooth, dark plating. It had been in interstellar space. It had been out there, away from warm beaches and warm sun, out where the cold was absolute, in the darkness between the stars. She touched it reverently, reaching up so that her fingers just barely grazed it at the lowest point where the hull curved down. It was cool even in the heat of the day.

"And this is Aurore," her father said proudly. "Aurore, can you shake the captain's hand?"

The big xalepos bent and took her hand very gently. "It is a pleasure."

She looked him in the eye. "I want to join your crew."

He and her father both laughed. "I think you are too young yet, Aurore," her father said.

"Come back in about twelve years if you want to apprentice," the captain said. "I can't take a four-year-old."

"Why not?" Aurore asked.

"You can't reach the control arm, for one thing." That seemed legit.

"I'll grow," Aurore promised.

For some reason they both laughed again. Her father picked her up, embroidered tunic scratchy against her arms, smelling of cologne instead of steel. "That's my girl," he said proudly. "Your great-grandfather built this fleet. These ships, and all the ships like them. He started out with nothing. And look what it's become!"

"Sixteen ships," the captain said. "And another keel laid on Lono. Every single one of us, kin or adopted, drawing good pay and living in nice apartments." He smiled at her. "And pretty clothes for little girls like you."

"I don't want pretty clothes," Aurore said firmly. "I want a starship."

"I'm the Heir of House Melian," her father said. "And you are my heir. You can have both. You can have everything, my darling."

Only everything came with responsibility. Her father worked twelve hours at a time, longer than any regular work shift, and certainly longer than a ship's watch. People were always pinging him during meals. He was always having to go somewhere, usually the port offices or a supplier or shipper or something.

Her mother's expression got tighter and tighter. "Helios, can't you tell them no this time?"

"It's House business," he said, and went.

She worked harder in school. She was first in her class. Someday she'd have to know how all of it was done. She'd need mathematics and hard sciences and all the things that made other students sweat. She was going to be the heir and a starship captain besides.

When she was ten, her mother moved into an apartment downstairs on the fifth floor. Her parents had decided to end their contract by mutual agreement. "Helios is married to his work," her mother said gently. "And I'm forty. I want something in my life besides clawing our way up. Haven't we come far enough?"

Probably not, Aurore thought. Everyone in the House was ok, but they only stayed that way as long as someone kept turning the wheel. And there were lots of people who weren't ok. She went to a school that wasn't expensive or exclusive, that took kids on scholarship along with ones who could pay. There were kids who wore old clothes and who didn't have enough to eat. There were kids who were Houseless. One girl wore the same thing every day and lived in a shipping container. Her mother was Merrow and she didn't have a father.

It bothered Aurore. She couldn't find her father that afternoon, so she moodily wandered into her grandfather's room. He lived in the same apartment on the tenth floor that he'd lived in for years, only now there were aides to help him because he couldn't walk very well. He was eighty-eight, weathered and reedy with blotched hands and was always glad to see her. She sat in the chair beside his drinking coffee with lots of milk and told him about it.

His dark eyes fixed on hers and he nodded slowly. "It's hard for the Merrow who come out of the desert," he said. "Powerful hard."

"I just feel bad for her," Aurore said. "Nobody will hire her mother because she's Merrow and it's not right."

The aide had gone on break, grateful that the granddaughter was there instead. "My mother was Merrow," he said abruptly.

Aurore's eyes widened. "What?"

"My mother," he said distinctly, "was Merrow. She was twenty-four years old when she ran."

"I've never heard this story," Aurore said.

He snorted. "Probably not. Helios knows how much harm it would do the business for people to think we were Merrow. There's a lot of prejudice, Aurore. But this is your story, and you've the right to know it." He put his cup down carefully on the little table. "The Merrow believe in strict segregation of the sexes. Men and women don't live together. When they're old enough, they're assigned a spouse who is genetically compatible. They see each other a few times a year on holy days and procreate."

"They don't have sex any other time?" Aurore asked incredulously.

"Not with someone of the opposite sex," her grandfather said. "They have to keep their population small. So instead of five genders like us, they have two. And those two can only mingle if they are married and then only a few times a year."

"I wouldn't like that," Aurore said decisively.

"Well, your great-grandmother didn't like it either. She was married and she saw him three times. And then he died. There was an accident of some kind. She didn't know what. He died. And so she could never marry again. She'd spend her life in celibacy unless she wanted a female lover. Which she didn't." He shrugged. "She wanted a husband and children. The Merrow

don't allow remarriage because it would cause bigamy in the afterlife. So she got together the supplies she'd need and she stole a trundle."

"Stole it?"

"She knew they'd track it, so she left in Full Night, when it was cool. She drove across the desert almost to the border of Tyria, south of us. Then she left the trundle and started going north. She knew, you see, that they'd find it and assume she was going to Tyria so they'd search between the trundle and Tyria, so she went the other way. She got onto the slopes of the Old Man before dawn."

"That's Beiran territory!" Aurore said.

"Just so." Her grandfather nodded. "So they didn't find her and take her back. She came to Beira and she lived in the slums, just like your friend. She met my father, who was navigations officer on a House Colon starship, because House Melian was nothing then. That was before our skirmish with the City of Tolema and he took a Tolema ship as a prize and got the prize captain's share. They took care of each other and they had me and your great-aunts. And she lived a long and happy life right here in this apartment." He looked around. "So you come by it honestly."

"Your father was a starship captain." That seemed amazing. "My great-grandfather."

"Oh yes." Her grandfather patted her knee. "Where do you think the first Melian ship came from? He took it from the Tolema. A boarding party, hand to hand, in orbit over the Great Southern Sea. He ran it himself twenty years. He married a Merrow widow and told everyone who didn't like it to piss up a tree."

Aurore laughed. "And no more living in shipping crates?"

Her grandfather waved one shaking hand around the room, warm and stuffed to the gills with antiques and readers, a big window with thick drapes open that looked upon the sea. "Does this look like a shipping crate? I built it myself after the last war. I built it all. And Helios will keep it. And so will you after him." He touched her cheek. "You've got it all. We're smart and bold and beautiful and shameless. Most of all we're lucky. The thing about luck is you've got to pass it on. I'll talk to Helios about finding a job for that friend of yours' mother."

"Would you?"

Her grandfather winked at her. "We stick together. Who knows? She could be your kin. We'll never know."

It wasn't much later that her friend came to school in new used clothes. Her mother had been hired by a restaurant kitchen. The restaurant belonged to a Melian cousin. Aurore didn't say anything about that. Power, she thought. This is what it's good for. At eleven years old she held it close. Power let you help people, even if they never knew what you did. She knew.

BEL PRESENTED himself at the Viceregal palace in midafternoon. He didn't have an appointment and professed himself disappointed that the Altissima was otherwise engaged while smiling to himself. Waiting for her to be free on what was doubtless a busy afternoon would mean that he had time to look about. "I understand that the gardens are exceptional," he said to the apologetic assistant who had explained that there had been some confusion with the schedule. "If you would direct me to them, I would be happy to take them in while the Altissima is busy. I have a great interest in gardens."

It was certainly a harmless request. He saw the assistant hesitate, weighing letting him roam about versus sitting in the assistant's office impatiently. How much trouble could he be strolling in the gardens? "Of course," the assistant said. "There are no less than three garden courtyards, each to a different theme. I hope you will enjoy them."

"I'm certain I shall," Bel said, gathering up his handheld as if he had a guidebook loaded. "I'm very enthusiastic about gardens."

"To be sure," the assistant said, and let him go his own way.

Bel wandered through the main gallery, looking for a door to the courtyard. Ah. It was certainly not locked. He stepped through and paused to take a breath.

The courtyard was large, its four radial paths offering a quick cut through for people passing from one part of the palace to another. At the center, where they met, there was a statue of the Lord of the Dance. He was not static or serene but caught in the moment of putting an arrow to his bow, feet apart and braced, a leaping hound at his feet frozen with its forefeet already off the ground, jumping to retrieve the prey he aimed at. A bird, no doubt. Surely it was a bird intended, not an evildoer. The Lord's bearded face was inscrutable. Whatever he did, it was without passion.

Bel approached. The statue was life-size. It stood encircled in empty troughs of dirt. Or perhaps they weren't empty, but merely waiting the touch of spring warmth to blossom into life. Each quadrant of the garden held a tree, benches beneath them. Spikes of flowers had begun to nose up through the dirt. In summer this would be an idyllic place. How many lovers had walked here? Or how many plotters?

He looked up. The palace was only two stories tall, second floor windows and balconies looking onto the garden just as the windows and doors did beneath. It was as Sura had said: every room would have needed a window when the palace was built originally, more than eight hundred years ago when there was no electrical power. Of course that had changed. Not every alteration was new. Lono had technology equal to Calpurnia's when they fell eighty years ago—equal technology, but not equal military might. Now they built the finest starships in the Nine Worlds, or at least everyone but the Morriganians thought so.

Bel strolled around the statue, taking in the pattern of the windows. There was the break. In the opposite corner from where he'd entered there were two windows on the second floor with none below them on the first. He could see the slight variance in the color of the stone on the first floor, as though windows had been blocked. That seemed a likely place for a secure room. So how to get to where the door must be? The door to the garden to the right of where he came in had promise. Hopefully it wasn't locked.

Bel strode to the door casually and opened it. What must have been another reception room had been divided into three with clear plasticene partitions, each with a modern screen desk behind it. Three people looked up from their work. "Good afternoon," Bel said courteously.

A young man looked up from the nearest desk. "Can I help you?"

"I'm Nereus Iulus," Bel said. "I'm afraid I've taken a wrong turn. Which office is this?" They would have heard of his claim. There were many offices he might plausibly be looking for.

The young man stood up, plain dark suit not a uniform but practically one, the cut and shade precisely marking his position in the civilian governmental hierarchy. "Of course," he said. "I can't give you full access but I can certainly show you the Autarch's office. But you understand I can't let you work there until the Altissima confirms it."

"Of course," Bel said courteously. The Autarch's staff. The Autarch's office. "I understand completely."

The young man led him down the room to the door at the far end beyond the assistants, who watched him curiously while trying not to seem to be doing so. He put a code in and opened the door, turning on the lights. The room was spacious, a screen desk at the far end, a group of conversation chairs grouped nearer the door, a low table between them. Glittering lamp stands stood in the corners and behind the conversation group. Screens lined the windowless walls around the desk, all dark. A cabinet stood midway down the wall, something glittering within. It lit automatically as Bel approached.

Black silk covered a model head, holding the crown aloft and allowing it to be seen from all angles as it should be, for it was not a simple circlet. The band was made of golden leaves attached to one another with fine-drawn wire, dozens of them to make a full wreath. On each side, long chains of golden leaves and berries dipped down to the wearer's shoulders, looping like the festival wreaths worn by celebrants, six strands intricate and lovely. Each leaf was perfect, beaten gold.

"The Solaste Crown," Bel said. It could be nothing else.

"He liked to look at it," the young man said. "It's beautiful, isn't it?"

"Very much so," Bel said. It was incredible. It was the kind of treasure that made a man's fingers itch. He wanted to touch it.

The young man glanced around the room. "So this is his office. He left everything tidy when he left for Cassandreia. He expected to be gone some time, naturally. He went directly to Calpurnia after the battle. And then…" He stopped, spreading his hands. "You know how he was killed by treachery."

"Yes," Bel said. He hadn't taken his eyes off the crown. How did the case open? Surely it did. If the Autarch had wanted it here, had he tried it on in private? Yes, he expected so. What else would a grim and gray Autarch do except try on a forbidden crown alone? After all, it was not his trophy. Lono had fallen before he was born. The crown must be a symbol of all he wished to be, not a prize of past victories. He reached for a crown and failed. Calpurnia had no crown. This crown was Lono's. It was a gift, freely given in love. Was that part of its secret?

Bel shook his head. Those were just old stories and none of his business anyway. His job was to get the crown. What Sura did with it after wasn't his problem. He turned away, making himself walk in front of the Autarch's desk. The screen was dark. He ran his hand along the intricate wooden edge. There was not one single item on the desk, nothing that provided any clue to the man who had used it.

"Moving in?"

Bel spun around. Altissima Antisia stood just inside the door. Today she wore a conservative dress suit of rich brown. "I was curious," Bel said simply. "I wanted to understand the Autarch better."

"He left nothing of himself here," she said.

"So I see."

Antisia took two steps toward him. "Except, apparently, you."

"Excuse me?"

She looked up at him, her eyes cool. "I have the results of the genetic test."

Bel kept his face smooth. "So soon? I'm surprised the dispatch boat has even had time to reach Calpurnia yet."

"The Autarch lived here for many years as Viceroy," Antisia said. "Of course our clinic had genetic samples from routine health procedures."

"I see." Bel schooled his voice while inwardly cursing Sura. Surely she should have thought of that!

Her mouth twitched. "The tests were positive. A 100 percent match. You are indeed the Autarch's son."

"What?" Bel was certain he'd misheard.

"You are the son of the Autarch Sanius Iulus," Antisia said, raising her chin. "Three different tests, each with a positivity rate in excess of 99 percent. There is no doubt. You are Nereus Iulus."

"But I..." Bel shut his mouth.

Her green eyes were surprisingly understanding. "It's a bit overwhelming, isn't it?"

"Yes, just a bit," Bel said. He tried to gather the threads of the plan. "I hoped, of course. But I didn't believe, if you know what I mean."

"I do," Antisia said. She looked sharply at the young assistant still hovering. "You have work, I expect."

"Yes, Altissima." He departed quickly, no doubt disappointed to miss the rest of the story. He'd tell the outer office within thirty seconds, Bel thought. Everyone in the palace would know in half an hour.

"I am going to give you one piece of advice, Nereus Iulus," Antisia said quietly. "And I will only give it once. Leave while you can. Nobody knows for certain except you and me. Rumors can be denied. Go and live a long and happy life. Your father..." She stopped and then went on. "Your father wanted to be Autarch because he wanted power and because he wanted to save Calpurnia from itself. It cannot be saved. He could not do it because we are simply too far gone. But you are not. You are free of the duties and obligations that bind me and that bound him. Your life is still your own. Run. Get off Lono and pretend you never heard this. If you wish, I will tell people that the genetic test was negative and that it was simply a mistake—you had hoped, but it proved untrue. I'll transfer some of Iulus' currency to you so that you have a substantial sum to get on with. And then you can go and make a life for yourself far away from here."

"I..." She was telling him to run, offering him currency to do it, currency for nothing that would give him a new stake. He could go. He could write this entire thing off as a deal gone strange, meet Aurore at her ship and lift for Menaechmi.

And never know.

In its case, the Solaste Crown glittered. It was waiting. It waited for the Blameless Prince. For the Calado heir. For the son of Amari Calado and the Autarch, that stern stranger who Antisia had been the true daughter to. The Autarch's heir.

"I can't do that," Bel said. "I need to understand."

Antisia let out a breath she'd been holding. "Then I will help you if I can," she said. Her eyes were frank. "We are both likely to die here. You are his true son. It is better to face what comes with honor rather than to flinch from the trial."

"I'm not prepared to die yet," Bel said.

THE AFTERNOON SUN was cutting through the low clouds, sunbeams warming the gardens of the Shrine, though the estuary was still hazed in a fog of pollution. Sura heard the sound of the electric vehicle and paused, the incense dipper in her hands. There was a stir within, raised voices. She waited. Bel plunged through the doors, the acolyte following after pleading that he was not expected and needed to be announced. "I need to talk to you," he said angrily.

Sura nodded serenely to the acolyte, though her hand clenched on the dipper. "Leave us," she said to the girl. The acolyte backed away, closing the doors behind her. Sura put the dipper down, folding her hands inside her opposite sleeves. It would not do for him to see them tremble.

"You knew." Bel's voice was sharp.

"Yes," Sura said simply.

"What in the name of the Lord's Balls is going on here?" Bel demanded. "Did you somehow suborn someone in the lab with the genetic test or is this true?"

"It is true," Sura said. She raised her head, standing beneath the budding apple tree, watching the man in his black Calpurnian suit, the basin of fire between them. "You are Nereus Iulus. You are Belimar Calado. You are the Blameless Prince."

He shook his head. "How can that be?"

"The documents I gave you were real. Thirty years ago, when he was a young man first assigned to Lono, Sanius Iulus had a child with a woman of Calado blood. He acknowledged the child privately and gave those documents to his son's mother. He assumed at that point that he would have other children, children of pure Calpurnian blood who would inherit his possessions there. He did not have so much on Lono then. He was not the Viceroy, merely an ambitious young man of twenty-nine." She looked at his face. "Younger than you are now."

Bel met her eyes. "You are Amari Calado."

"Yes," Sura said. She would not feel her heart, not here at this moment.

He took a deep breath. "And my mother? My mother who raised me? On Adelpha?"

"Nysia was an acolyte here at the Shrine. She knew you from babyhood and loved you. When it became too dangerous for you to stay here, she volunteered to take you with her to Adelpha as her own child. It is clear she raised you with love." Sura's voice broke on the last word.

"And you?" he asked angrily. "What kind of game is this?"

"I wanted you to live."

Bel paced away, looking out over the estuary. A starship inbound to Tranquility cut through the scudding clouds above, the sound of its engines following after.

"I do not expect you to forgive me," Sura said.

"I'm not sure what you've done yet," Bel said. "Why don't you start at the beginning?" His eyes were clear now, cool and calculating another move in the game. Of course. What else had she and Sanius been, if not cold? And she could see him here, another young man in perfectly tailored black, tall and lean, dark-skinned and handsome.

"I was younger then than you are now," Sura said. "The Calado had fallen fifty years before. I was from a cadet line, raised here at the Shrine as Sura. I was expected to live out my life here. Given to the Lord of the Dance, I would be a tidy end to the royal line. I was simply a girl, unambitious and harmless."

Bel snorted. "Or not."

"Or not," Sura agreed. "But I could see how hopeless rebellion was. Every day I could stand here and see the reasons." She gestured to the flare of fire in the haze below, the starship's boosters taking the weight of the ship as it sunk onto one of Tranquility's landing pads. "My parents had been killed leading a rebellion that did nothing except that seven hundred people died and the Calpurnians shook it off, a week's news at home. I was young and I wanted to live. I didn't want to be a sad song. Beautiful Amari, the doomed rose of Lono? I wanted so much more." She took a deep breath.

"And so you decided to conceive a child with the Autarch," Bel said.

Sura shook her head. The clouds were clearing above, the superstructure of the capital ship in low orbit glittering. "No. I fell in love with the enemy." She didn't look at him. "He came to the Shrine to pay his respects, he said. The Lord of the Dance had been one of the principal gods of Calpurnia, but people there no longer believed. He sought Mystery. He found it here." Her voice dropped. "He went into the heart of the maze and he found what he sought."

"And he found you."

"I was his guide. Someone must be. It is the story." She looked at him, for it seemed that he shivered. "You will understand."

"I expect so," Bel said wryly.

"But what is love compared to the fates of empires? It is nothing." Sura took a deep breath. "Not quite two years. He was ordered to shipboard service. He made the declaration in your favor as you have seen, when you were four months old. And he left." She looked at Bel. "Remember, he was not the Autarch then. He was a young man of good family, of Senatorial family. He was ambitious. He was not about to wreck those ambitions." She let her eyes linger on his face. "You have no idea what it is to love a child until it is yours. You have no idea what it truly means to love someone more than yourself." Bel nodded slowly. "You stayed here until you were nearly three. And then there was a new Viceroy, one who promised a crackdown on Lonoi independence movements. It was too dangerous. I sent you off Lono with Nysia."

Bel looked around. "I lived here as a young child," he said. His eyes roved over the basin, over the garden just flushing with spring. "It seemed like a dream. But it was because I had been here before." He raised his chin. "Did you ever see him again?"

"Yes." Sura's voice didn't shake. "Eight years ago he became Viceroy of Lono. He came to the Shrine. I told him I didn't know where you were. Which at that point I did not. You had left the university on Calpurnia. I had no idea where you were or what you were doing."

"I was here on Lono," Bel said. Sura whipped around to look at him. "I was here," Bel said. "I came back to Lono after I dropped out. I got involved in some schemes. One of them was Lonoi Resistance."

"Oh Bel," Sura said, and she gripped the edge of the plinth the fire basin stood on.

"I had this crazy idea that Lono ought to rebel against Calpurnia," Bel said. "We plotted to blow up Calpurnian facilities, sabotage ships and things like that. We drank a lot and sang a lot of sad songs." He shrugged. "I got out after a plan went bad. We weren't going to win. We were just going to get a lot of people killed. It did more harm than good." He met her eyes. "I was tasked with assassinating a Calpurnian official. I said I was out. I may be a lot of things, but I'm not an assassin." Sura closed her eyes. "I left Lono."

She had known about the rising wave. She had seen the executions on the nets, saboteurs who had blown up part of the Yards, eight Calpurnians and thirteen Lonoi killed. And she had never dreamed… And yet she knew how the tragedies went, the ones that unleashed the Hounds: a young man doesn't know who his father is and kills him, an unwitting parricide. Bel had turned away from that not because he knew, but because he simply thought assassination was wrong. Sura opened her eyes. "You are the Blameless Prince."

"I don't believe in the Blameless Prince," Bel said sharply.

"If you are not, then who?" She put her head to the side. "If you refuse your destiny and walk away, who will take it up?

"I do not have a destiny!" he snapped. "That's nothing but a fable. Look, this is all too much. Belimar Calado. Nereus Iulus. Which am I anyway?"

"You are both," Sura said.

"That is completely impossible and you know it!" Bel shouted. "It was impossible to begin with!"

"Don't you think I knew that?" Sura shouted back, her composure leaving her. "Don't you think we both knew how impossible it was?

But are we all playthings? Nothing but leaves in a fast-moving stream? Part of the inevitable march of history controlled by economic and social forces that simply carry us along? Or do we believe that those with strength and wit can swim against the current? Can control the current with dams and bridges and culverts?"

"History is not made by great people," Bel said. "It's made by social forces beyond anyone's control."

"History is made by you right this moment," Sura countered. "If you choose to walk away, you have chosen. Not social forces. You. Bel. It's up to you." She took a deep breath, trying to be cool. "You can choose to be Belimar or Nereus or both or neither. But whatever you choose, you did it. It's not inevitable or vast social forces or anything else. You choose, just like we did." She blinked furiously. "And maybe we chose badly. But we chose. We are not victims, Sanius and I. We were never victims in anything we did."

She heard his step behind her. "The Altissima said I should run." He took another step, nearly beside her. "She said Thurinia is coming and that she will crush the Altissima's forces. She expects to die. And everyone who stands with her." Bel sat down on the edge of the plinth next to her. "I knew Social Logic adherents on Adelphi and Calpurnia. Altissima Gnea was the most visible, but Thurinia and others followed her. Lots of people believe in Social Logic—sanity, health and rationality. I can't live that way. Neither can a lot of other people. I ran."

Sura looked at him sideways. "It seems you've been doing a lot of running. When are you going to stand?"

"There's no point in standing against the inevitable."

Her eyes held his. "You are the Blameless Prince. If you don't stand, who will?"

He didn't look away. "I'm not a warrior. I'm a con man, a gambler."

"Then maybe you'd better start looking for some cards up your sleeve," Sura said. "Because whether you stay or not, Thurinia is going to crush Lono and Altissima Antisia both, the last Calpurnian faction that held out against her. We can't all run." She took a deep breath. "And we're done with running. The Rising is upon us."

Bel shook his head incredulously. "No."

"We have been waiting for a moment of Calpurnian weakness.

When do you think they have ever been weaker? Altissima Antisia is barely standing on her feet. Her fleet is in ruins. If there were ever a chance for a Rising to succeed, now is the time."

"If Lono rises against the Calpurnians now, all we will do is be crushed by Thurinia," Bel said. "It's not that I oppose Lonoi independence. I fought for it. But I won't just get people killed needlessly."

"Then now is the time to rise!" Sura said. "Now, when Calpurnia is battered by the Morriganians and civil war between factions alike. Antisia can't stop it."

"Antisia is the least of the problems," Bel said. "We could do worse. Thurinia and Social Logic are worse."

"Perhaps so, but they are not here."

"They will be," Bel said. His eyes were utterly honest. "If we rebel, we will take Antisia down and then Thurinia will be unopposed. She will retake Lono savagely. She will be Autarch. She will rebuild her fleet here and bring Menaechmi to heel. Thousands will die and it will be generations before we have another chance."

Sura felt her heart beat faster. "I can't stop it," she said. She got up, pacing around the Image. "I'm not the leader. I don't even know who most of the cell leaders are. My task was to find you and secure the Solaste Crown. Bel, I can't call off the Rising. It will happen whether you participate or not."

"With or without your Blameless Prince as a figurehead," Bel said. There was a bitter trace in his voice. "Not as necessary as I seemed, am I?"

"Bel…"

"I need to think," Bel said. He got to his feet. "I can't…" He hesitated. He didn't reach for her. "I'll be in touch."

Sura watched him leave. She waited until she heard the sound of the electric engine before she sank to her knees on the damp ground, blind with tears. "Dark Lord," she whispered. "I have failed."

CHAPTER
SIX

AURORE WENT into the port offices of Mari Brothers for her afternoon appointment. Her usual black cargo pants and jacket caused no remark here; Calpurnian codes of dress more or less stopped at the gates to the Yards. Besides, Tenn Mari was Innocent. He wasn't properly Calpurnian or Lonoi either.

And because of that, business meetings had to be preceded with tea and small talk, which Aurore found a comforting ritual. She could cope with Calpurnian brusqueness, but the niceties of the negotiation were her cultural baggage as well as his. Tenn was a burly man in his sixth decade, head shaven as many of the Innocent did to better show the tattoo of leaping flame above his right eyebrow. They were marked with a god-sign as coming of age, he'd said once. His god was the Artifix, entirely appropriate to a starship engineer, and one of the best.

The tea service was metal and glass, not pottery, simple and graceful in design, served at a table in his office, its built-in screen darkened. "And how is your family?" Tenn asked. "Your esteemed father?"

"A father once again, or soon will be," Aurore said. "I am to have a new sister in the coming year."

"My felicitations," Tenn said politely. "Does this welcomed child have a name?"

"She will be Selena Melian," Aurore said. It was important to make it clear she was born with full House-right, Melian rather than Sardai i Melian, since Caralys was a gaura rather than a contracted wife.

"An ancient and fortunate name," Tenn said. He lifted his little glass cup. It looked like a soap bubble in his strong fingers. He turned it round, looking at it rather than at her. "I'm sorry about the missiles."

"Tenn, we've paid for them," Aurore said.

"It's not just that the Altissima said no," he said. He regarded the cup as though it might tell him something. "You've been down the line in the Yards."

"There are some pretty damaged ships," Aurore said cautiously. Mari Brothers was generally scrupulous about not discussing one client's work with another.

"They're blown all to pieces," Tenn said bluntly, meeting her eyes. "Two of them should be scrapped, and that's my professional opinion. Instead, the Altissima says to tape them back together any way we can. And that's on her, if she wants to send crews into space on systems in danger of catastrophic failure, but I've told her there's only so much I can do, and it's true of the other fitters too. But we're screwed if Thurinia and the Social Logic people take over, so what can we do?"

Aurore frowned. "Why is one set of Calpurnians worse than the other?"

"Because this set has pretty much left the Innocent alone, and the Social Logic people won't." Tenn took a quick sip of his tea. "Look, we're not Lonoi. After the Righteous War we were liberated from debt-servitude on Inanna. We're the Innocent. The victims. The perpetrators were Isolated and we were given a new home here on Lono." He shrugged. "It was good for everybody. The Lonoi didn't like tech and think it's spiritually polluting. We'd spent our lives working in factories and operating tech. We moved here and we were the bosses. You look at it now, something like 80 percent of the highest paying jobs in Tranquility are held by Innocent. Some Calpurnians, a few Lonoi, but mostly us. We're medics and engineers. The Calpurnians know the economy would collapse without us. Who'd build starships and drones? The Lonoi? Half of them think it's morally superior to wash dishes without a machine! They sweep their floors with brooms instead of just letting the vac do it."

"To each their own," Aurore said. There were techs that were illegal on Menaechmi too, things people had figured out caused more problems than they solved.

"That's what I say," Tenn said. "So up until now, the Calpurnians have mostly left us alone culturally. We recognize three genders instead of two and stuff like that. The Calpurnians only have male and female, though you can change between. They don't recognize non-binary as a gender. And neither do the Lonoi. The Lonoi don't even allow sex between people of the same gender. If it was up to them, we'd have to follow their laws, and they hate it that we don't. The Calpurnians let us make our own laws for our own community. Or have. Social Logic people think they have some kind of universal principle. I tell you, when Altissimus Iulus was Viceroy he didn't care who had which genitals or who anybody slept with! And Altissima Antisia doesn't care either." He shook his head. "But get some Social Logic Viceroy in here, and we're squeezed between them and the Lonoi? Gonna suck for us."

"The Golden Lady of Menaechmi has repudiated the Isolation," Aurore said cautiously. Or rather, her father had on the Golden Lady's behalf. "Why don't you go back to Inanna?"

Tenn looked at her like she was crazy. "Go back? We were rescued from there generations ago! Nobody living has ever been anywhere near Inanna! A bunch of inbred, vicious barbarians descended from corporate tyrants? We're not Inannan. We're nothing like them. We're descendants of their victims."

"Surely nobody on Inanna now was ever a corporate tyrant," Aurore said. "It was a long time ago."

"A hundred and fifty years. That's how long we've been here. This is our home," Tenn said. "Our community. Our way of life. And we have Calpurnians who want to live here because it's better. I'll flat out say that our way of life is freer and better than either the Lonoi or the Calpurnian. Isn't that worth preserving?"

"It is indeed," Aurore said. She refrained from saying that surely it would not survive if not for the Lonoi who worked the shit jobs in the

Yards and who cooked the food and washed the dishes. But then if they didn't think it was morally acceptable to use technology, what could you do with that? It was like the Merrow, she thought. They used technology, but they required complete separation of the genders. Well, every world has these problems. It's human nature. "But back to my refit…"

"I get why the Altissima is holding onto the missiles," Tenn said. "It isn't much, but it's what she's got. If Thurinia had any idea how screwed this fleet is, Lono would fall in five minutes."

"Then we'll just hope she doesn't find out," Aurore said.

THE RESTAURANT FLOATED in the estuary, only a long walkway connecting it to one of the permanent docks, a little artificial island of glass and steel with windows all around. They had a private room that looked out to sea, curtains drawn to show an expanse of sky and the distant horizon. Two thick dark blue cushions were set side by side at a long, low table, the burner in the center of it keeping the broth hot while they ate. A quiet server laid a platter of vegetables and seafood for them to select from, a set of wooden skewers to hold them in the broth, and then departed.

Antisia poured herself a cup of peach wine, but Dian demurred. "I'm trying not to, thanks."

Antisia's's eyebrows rose. "You drank the other night."

Dian shrugged nonchalantly. "I have a drinking problem. So I try not to get started and hold myself to just one. It's fun to get messed up, but not all the time."

Antisia looked down at her cup. "I would do the same, but I don't think it really matters at this point."

"It might matter if you'd like to be conscious later," Dian pointed out.

"It might at that." She set the cup on the table. Dian was heady as fruit wine. She'd like to remember the sex.

"You seem on edge tonight," Dian said. She pushed back her hair, the ends tipped in blue. Tonight she wore a shirt with cascading ruffles of chiffon down the front, enough to conceal but hint at what was beneath, a shade of gray-blue the color of the stormy sky. A pendant of ruddy gold in the shape of some fantastic animal hung between her breasts. She was everything that was not Calpurnian gravitas, alluring and unique. "Do you never see the same woman twice?"

"It's not you," Antisia said. "Believe me, I'm delighted to be here." She frowned at her cup but didn't lift it.

Dian raised an eyebrow. "So is there someone you're cheating on?"

"What? No." She took a drink from her cup, letting the peach wine linger in her mouth. "If I were in a serious relationship, I wouldn't cheat. I don't have serious relationships."

"Why not?" Dian gestured at her. "You're passable."

Antisia laughed, as no doubt Dian had meant her to. "Small praise."

"You're good in bed. You've been sexing somebody. So why not a relationship?"

She took another deep drink. Why not be honest? There was no danger in it, not now. All of the consequences didn't matter. "I'm only interested in women."

"So? It doesn't seem that's a problem on Calpurnia."

"It's not. I mean, there's not a problem with having sex with someone who has the same genitals you do. But I'm in the Navy, and I never stay anywhere long enough to meet women who aren't in the Navy unless they're inappropriate. All of the women in the Navy are just like me." She turned her cup round and round. "Driven. Professional. Climbing. I don't find looking in the mirror very attractive." She glanced up at Dian, the anthesis of all of it, lounging on the pillows with her blue-tipped hair. "I find you much more interesting."

Dian's mouth quirked to the side. "I'm soft *xalepia*, not all the way to *hapalia*. But surely there are *hapalia* women on Calpurnia? You can't all be hard *xalepia*."

Antisia sighed. "I'm not completely sure what you mean by that."

"Soft, pretty women with long hair and flowing clothes and sparkly makeup?"

"You mean plebs," Antisia said. "The only people who dress like that, whatever their gender is, are plebians. Bright colors, long hair, skirts instead of trousers—they're plebians. Servants. Workers. They lack gravitas." She took a breath, but it probably wouldn't shock Dian the way it would most people. "I've done that a few times—sexed prostitutes. I couldn't possibly have a relationship with a plebian. To start with, I'm an Altissima. It couldn't truly be consensual because I could destroy her life with a word. Consent can only be possible between people with exactly the same status, income and power. So the more power you have, the more it becomes impossible to have a relationship."

Dian picked up her cup and took a tiny sip. She didn't look shocked at all. "That's a problem," she said. "Why do you do it? I mean, why do people?"

"We have complete equality between the sexes," Antisia said. "Your genes or your genitals have nothing do to with your social role. If you're good enough, you can succeed and excel and rule. Scientists, mathematicians, engineers, soldiers, all the professions are open to you regardless of your gender. If you're tough and unemotional."

Dian looked at her over the rim of the cups. "What about the arts?"

"We don't have them. Not really. Performance is illegal. Music is recorded and has to be distributed with no identifier of the musician so they can't be exploited."

"Vids? Painting? Advertising?" Dian was incredulous. "I know I've seen visual art."

"But not of real people." Antisia's cup was empty and she refilled it. "It's illegal to exploit any person by making images of them. All the art you've seen is computer generated. There are no actresses or models or singers. All of those were means of exploiting women. Since the Politists came in, all of that has been illegal."

"Fuck that," Dian said. "No wonder Calpurnian vids are so boring."

Antisia caught her breath and then started laughing. "You would say anything, wouldn't you?"

"And you would think it but not say it," Dian said. She lounged back on the pillow. "But you're a Federationist, not a Politist, right?"

"The Autarch was a Federationist," Antisia said. "And I was his protégé. So yes, Federationist. But the Federationists lost power after the Lindorn Massacre eighty years ago. Altissimus Iulus was the first

Autarch to be a Federationist since then. But that's over, and Social Logic is the real challenge to the Politists now."

"And they're crazy?"

Antisia sighed. "I suppose they're a reaction to both the Federationists and the Politists."

"Is it always politics?" Dian asked.

"Always," Antisia said. "You have no idea how much I'd like to be free of it." For some reason her eyes seemed to be misted. "I have worked my entire life—literally since I was four years old—for this position, and I can't... I can't do this anymore." *Cornelia*'s command center swam before her eyes and she closed them. "I am flawed. I've lost virtue, gravitas... I can't do this."

"Then stop," Dian said.

Antisia laughed mirthlessly. "How? I can't just quit."

"Why not?" She opened her eyes. Dian was leaning on one shoulder as though she expected a couch instead of pillows. "Surely it's possible to retire from the Calpurnian Navy."

"Well, yes. But what would I do then? Assuming Thurinia didn't kill me, which is a big assumption." She lifted the cup then. "I have no desire to ever set foot on a starship again, and that's the only thing I know how to do besides fight. And I have no desire to fight either. You seem to think I can just reinvent myself as something new."

"Why not?" Dian asked. "People do it all the time."

"On Menaechmi, maybe," Antisia allowed, taking another drink.

Dian leaned on her shoulder. "Close your eyes," she said quietly.

"All right." Antisia closed them, feeling the tips of Dian's hair brush against her sleeve.

"It's evening," Dian said softly. "And you're sitting on a dual lounger with me, looking up at the vines that make up the arbor above us, twined with tiny lights. There's a soft breeze and the scent of the ocean flowing against us. You can feel the warmth radiating from the wall behind the arbor, a terracotta wall that runs around the rooftop on two sides, the sides that aren't glass doors into the building. There's a firepit and light leaping in it, candles all around, lights on strings over a couple of little tables, and other loungers in corners dark enough that no one can see. There's the sound of voices. Just a few people, talking.

There's the sound of a child telling a long story. You can hear the flames in the firepit. You can smell the flowers on the arbor, sweet and intoxicating. You can see the stars appearing as the sun goes down into the sea. Up here, even the sounds of the city are muted. Everything seems far away. Except for my arm around you."

There was the warmth of Dian's arm, a slow and sultry kiss against her neck. Antisia opened her eyes, turned her head and leaned into it. After a moment she pulled back. "How did you do that?" she asked. "That felt real."

"It is a real place." Dian sat up, her eyes sparkling, taking a sip of her soup instead of wine. "That's the roof at home, House Melian in Beira."

"You made it feel like I was there," Antisia said.

"Empathy is a common gift on Menaechmi," Dian said, reaching for one of the skewers and shoving it through a crustacean to put in the hot broth. "There's more than a little of it in my family. Not just anybody can be Husband of the Golden Lady."

"Pardon?"

"My father is the Husband of the Golden Lady. It's complicated." Dian put the skewer in the hot pot. "I must say, it's nice to go out with someone who hasn't seen my father's scrotum."

Antisia choked on her wine. "What?"

"On the nets. They do like to linger at the Royal Wedding." Dian put a tiny dollop of sauce on her plate. "Personally, I always find it a bit weird."

"I thought your father was a merchant prince, not a…" Antisia searched for a nice way of saying *actor in obscene films*.

"He is." Dian smirked. "That's why he's Husband of the Golden Lady."

"I don't understand at all," Antisia said bemusedly. "But that place… You love it."

"Of course I do," Dian said simply. "Beira's a mess and House Melian is a beehive full of very nutty bees. And that's not the whole house, just the ones who live in the building."

Antisia was confused. "How many people live in your house?"

Dian put her head to the side. "A hundred and thirty-four in the building, I think. There are another nine hundred and six with full House membership and a couple of thousand with partial rights—you know, people who belong to another House but they've moved in with a contracted partner—things like that."

"I meant your family," Antisia said.

"That is my family." Dian fished the crustacean out, now bright pink, and slathered it with sauce, her dark blue fingernails picking it up delicately from the skewer. "It will be a hundred and thirty-five when my little sister's born. The newest one. You'd think we had enough Melians, but apparently not. My father's gaura is pregnant, which is one reason I got sent on this trip. I think he thought Aurore and I would be too upset after the way things happened when Mia was born. Or maybe he just wanted us out of the way so he could have big feelings all by himself." Dian shrugged. "Either way. I'll have a new sister. I'm not really a baby person, are you?"

"I understood approximately half of that," Antisia said. "And I don't know. I've never been around a baby. Of course I've never met anyone who was pregnant. We don't do that."

Dian spoke very slowly, as though to someone dim. "Then where do more little Calpurnians come from?"

"Surrogates. Patrician women bank their eggs when they're twenty or so in case they ever want to be genetic parents. If you decide you want to in thirty years, you get a surrogate."

"No one ever carries a baby?" Her voice was incredulous.

"It's unpleasant, a risk to your health, and interrupts your career in its critical phases. Why would anyone do that?" And yet Dian seemed perplexed. "Is there some value in the experience?"

"Don't they take care of their kids?"

"Of course. I had around the clock nannies and I saw my parents nearly weekly," Antisia said. "They're nice enough people. We have an appropriate relationship."

Dian waved her cup around in the air. "I mean, like washing them and feeding them and playing stupid games with them. Or wiping up your grandpa's drool and listening to him tell you the same story forty-nine times. Don't you take care of people?"

Antisia thought she was fishing for something. "Those jobs are done by professionals. By people who have received a certificate in the appropriate caregiving area."

"Plebians," Dian said flatly.

"Of course," Antisia said. "Caregiving isn't really brain work, not the way the sciences or finance is. It's not really possible to do anything except what I've been doing if you want to succeed. You have to focus on work every day, all day. You can't be self-indulgent and disappoint people or not live up to your potential by losing opportunities based on personal preferences." She blinked. For some reason the world seemed a little out of focus. She hadn't drunk that much yet, had she? "It doesn't matter if you enjoy it or not."

Dian looked at her with something like pity in her eyes. "Surely there's something you enjoy doing that isn't work."

Antisia blinked. "I suppose," she said slowly. "I haven't thought about it in a long time."

"Well? What do you like to do?"

"I like to run," Antisia said. She remembered that. "I did a lot of long-distance running when I was in school. We were out in the country and there were trails. But now I just run on the treadmill the required hours for exercise."

"I like to run too," Dian said. "And hike. I like the trails on the Old Man—that's our active volcano—and in the mountains further north. I spent a lot of time up there a couple of years ago. My dad decided that I needed to get out of Beira so I wouldn't party so much, and there are farms up near Amphi that House Melian bought in my grandfather's day, so I got sent up there to learn the business." Dian shrugged. "I actually liked it. Viticulture is interesting. And while a lot of what we grow is corn, corn, corn, there are peach and apricot orchards too. There are roads where you can just run and run without seeing another human being. Just trees and fields and mountains and sky."

"That sounds beautiful." She paused, then said thoughtfully, "I like the outdoors. I used to enjoy things like that."

Dian nibbled on the crustacean. "So visit Menaechmi."

"I can't do that," Antisia said. For some reason it made her chest hurt.

"Because you're planning to die here."

"Yes," Antisia said.

THEY WENT BACK to her suite after dinner, and she made love to Dian as though it were the last time. It was a gift, a few days of light before the end. *Most people don't know,* Antisia thought, coming down from the peak. *They know the first time, but they don't know the last. They go about their lives and never see the blow coming, or they pretend that it will be all right, say goodbye assuring someone that they'll be back. I know this is the last. This is the last time I will touch someone. This is the last time I will fall into her.*

Afterwards, she turned her face against the pillows, and Dian snugged the comforter around them. She slid her arms around her from behind, her face against Antisia's shoulder. "There, Victoria," she said.

Antisia squeezed her eyes shut. "I should take you home," she said. "Tomorrow morning you'll have your missiles. You should raise ship immediately."

"Eager to be rid of me now?" Dian's voice was light. And yet this was serious.

She lifted her head. "I mean it," she said bluntly. "You wanted numbers? I'll give you numbers. Thurinia has ten ships in spaceworthy condition, fully armed and battle ready. I have one. I have one additional ship that is spaceworthy and four with big holes in them. She has approximately 300 missiles. I have nineteen and you have six. Now, it's true she won't bring all ten of her best ships with her. She'll leave some to guard Calpurnia. Let's say she brings six. That's six on one, 180 missiles to nineteen. How do you think that battle will come out? She's going to roll over us. If I'm lucky and if I have the courage to do it, I might be able to take her out in a suicide attack. It's likely I won't succeed. I've dismissed my crews except for those who refuse to go. We will be all volunteers. And we are going to die. So you need to leave now." She met Dian's eyes solidly. "You are wonderful and beautiful and this has been the most amazing interlude. I hope you will remember me kindly." She stopped. There was no way to go on.

Dian's face was oddly blank. Stricken, perhaps. Or simply shocked.

She didn't say something ridiculous about how she could stay and fight. Obviously that was stupid. Adding one lightly armed Menaechman merchanter would make no difference. It would simply get Dian and her crew killed.

Antisia reached up, brushing Dian's hair back from her eyes. "Please go," she said.

Dian nodded. Was it Antisia's imagination that there were tears in her eyes?

"You'll have the missiles before midday," Antisia said. "Go back to your beautiful world and raise a glass to me at sunset. And be happy. You deserve to be happy."

Dian gulped. Then she kissed her hard, kissed her as Antisia's eyes overflowed, tangling and drowning once more.

It was late when Bel stepped off the tram at the entrance to Tranquility Yards, the moons both setting behind the sea cliffs. The stars were pale, barely visible through the smog in the valley. He had his duffel over his shoulder, and his blue wrap coat made him nondescript. He might be any worker reporting early for a morning launch, rather than Nereus Iulus. *Golden Wanderer* was quiet, and he hesitated for a moment before he hit the courtesy chime. Probably they were sleeping and wouldn't appreciate a passenger arriving suddenly. And yet the longer he wandered around Tranquility, the more likely he'd get stuck in something. Best to get aboard and lie low. He hit the chime.

To Bel's surprise, Aurore opened the hatch almost immediately. She was fully dressed and frowning. "Oh," she said flatly, "it's you."

"Who were you hoping for?" Bel said as he came aboard.

"Dian. I expected her back hours ago. She had an assignation."

Bel followed her into the common room and dropped his duffel on the floor. "How soon do you think you can raise ship after she arrives?"

Aurore's eyebrows rose. "So you got the crown and delivered it?"

Bel sat down heavily in one of the chairs. "Not exactly," he said. "Do you have any coffee?"

"I can make some," Aurore said. He heard her fiddling with the packets as he rested his head in his hands. "So you didn't get the crown and now you're wanted?"

"Not that either." It seemed frankly unbelievable. Yet hours of walking around Tranquility and thinking had brought no clarity, just tired repetition of unbelievable facts.

"What then?" There was the smell of coffee as the brewer worked.

"I'm Nereus Iulus," he said.

Aurore turned to look at him quizzically. "No, you're not."

"I am. Nereus Iulus. Belimar Calado. I just found out." His head was splitting.

Aurore put two mugs of coffee down on the table and sat down. "I thought you were pretending to be Nereus Iulus and that you worked for the Lonoi Resistance."

Oh right. He'd said that. "The Lonoi Resistance hired me to get the Solaste Crown and to pretend to be Nereus Iulus, the son of the Autarch and Amari Calado. They told me not to be worried about a genetic sample because I'd be gone before the results came back. Thing is, they knew the results would be positive. They knew I really am—him." Bel lowered his head over the steaming mug.

"They who?"

"Amari Calado." He couldn't bring himself to say 'my mother.' His mother was Nysia.

"So you were pretending to be someone not knowing that you actually are him?" Aurore sounded skeptical.

"That's the size of it." He looked up. "And now I'm totally screwed."

"Because you don't have the crown?"

"I don't want to be Nereus Iulus! Or Belimar Calado! Or anybody else!" Bel said. "I am not their Blameless Prince! And I certainly don't want to lead some rebellion that's going to get a lot of people killed and not achieve anything." He took a drink, wincing at the heat, and put the mug down abruptly. "Every generation or so there's a Rising. And it ends the same way—thousands of people killed, thousands more losing their homes or jobs, and nothing changes. It is absolutely impossible to take on Calpurnia in a rebellion and win. They have the ships, the soldiers, and enough ordnance to blow up the planet. To steal the Solaste Crown and hide it, ok. Sure. We can do stuff like that. But the idea that I'm going to lead a rebellion against Altissima Antisia and her fleet and win? It's laughable. I'm not a soldier. I'm not a leader. Even with the damage they've taken from Morrigan, it's ridiculous. All that will happen is that I will get a bunch of idealistic kids killed. I won't do it. If they want to do this, they'll do it without me. I'm out of here."

"It sounds to me you're thinking like a responsible leader," Aurore said, "if you're more concerned with the people who might follow you than your own ambition."

Bel stared at her. "What do you know about how responsible leaders think?"

Aurore leaned back in her chair. "I think I know quite a lot. I've been raised to be one my entire life. Heir of House Melian, remember? I've watched good leaders and bad ones since I was a kid, and I've always known that one day I was going to have to make the big decisions whether I wanted to or not. You don't get to choose who your parents are. You just don't. If responsibility is what you get, then you have to use it well. Anything else hurts people."

"I…" Bel began.

"That doesn't fit your picture of a Menaechman merchant House?" Aurore lifted her mug. "We may preen and look weak to you, but I have the utmost respect for my father, the Guardian of Beira, and how he's kept us safe and helped us prosper. And yes, I'd much rather be a ship's captain. The gods know I'm badly suited to being his heir! But it will be my responsibility to keep House Melian safe someday, unless somebody else can do it better. So if you're the Blameless Prince, you'd better start thinking about what you can do to keep Lono safe. That's your job."

"I don't…" Bel began, then stopped.

"Well?"

"I suppose I must seem self-indulgent to you," he said slowly. "I'm used to my life being my own."

"It's not," Aurore said.

"That's what Sura said." Bel cupped his hands around his mug.

"She said that anything I did was a choice, even if I ran away. That's a choice. There is nothing I can do that won't matter."

Aurore raised an eyebrow. "Don't you ever play games? Everything you do affects the endstate."

"It's not a game."

"No. But games teach us something counter to the Social Logic narrative. Everything you do matters. Every choice everyone makes matters. There are no people whose actions are zero-sum." She leaned forward. "Some of us can see more clearly how we matter."

"Sura said that right now it was all on me either way." Bel took a deep breath. "This Rising is going to happen. I can steer it or choose not to. But there's no way that the results aren't on me either way."

"So what do you think should happen?" Aurore asked. Her face was kind now. She had something hard about her, but not cruel. Her eyes were gentle.

He looked down at the coffee in the mug. "I think if there is a Rising it will come closer than any has in years because they're right: Calpurnia is weak now. But Antisia can still beat our asses, and if she doesn't, the main fleet will arrive to put the rebellion down. They're not going to let Lono go. It's not like Menaechmi. There are a lot of Calpurnians who live here. And that's another thing. I'm not in favor of the kind of bloodshed there will be. They're here because this is a better place to live than Calpurnia. There's more freedom and a lot more opportunity. They don't deserve to die for wanting a better life. I left because I wanted a freer life!" He looked up. "I don't know how to do this. I'm not one or the other. I'm both."

"I understand," Aurore said. "You're Belimar Calado and Nereus Iulus at the same time. The Blameless Prince and the Autarch's heir."

Bel opened his mouth and then shut it again. "Wait," he said. An idea. Just an idea. But it was the kind of brilliant stroke that opened everything. "What if instead of putting down the Rising, Antisia recognized it? What if she recognized Nereus Iulus as the ruler of Lono? She can't recognize Belimar Calado, but she could defer to Nereus Iulus."

"Can she do that?" Aurore asked.

"All his possessions on Lono. That's what the declaration said." Bel's voice rose. He had something here. "At the time he was twenty-nine and that wasn't much. But now—he was the Viceroy when he died. What if the Blessed Prince and the Viceroy were the same person? Altissima Antisia could recognize him. We wouldn't have to fight each other. I'd recognize her command, and she'd recognize me as Viceroy. The Resistance would accept Belimar Calado." The pattern was beautiful. "That's what Sura meant. Or what somebody meant. If I'm both, then there doesn't have to be a war."

"Maybe it's what the Lord of the Dance meant," Aurore said quietly.

"I don't know anything about that," Bel said. It made him uncomfortable, and yet the Image came into his mind, burned face watching him. Burned when the Calpurnians took Tranquility, eighty years ago, restored and damaged at once.

"Are the other Factions going to recognize you as Viceroy?" Aurore asked.

"Of course not." It was all fitting, like drawing to the inside in a game of cards. "But we'll have Antisia's fleet. If she's with us instead of against us, then her Faction and Lono can stand against Thurinia's faction or any of the other smaller ones. We can do this." He looked at her. "We can actually free Lono without killing or exiling every person with Calpurnian blood."

"Which would include you."

"Yes." It was stunning in its simplicity. "I need to go back to the Shrine. I need to talk to Sura." He got to his feet.

Aurore smiled. "Then go," she said. "And let me know how it comes out."

He stopped. "Thank you," he said. "I don't..."

"I didn't do anything," Aurore said.

"You did but..." He couldn't quite find the words for it. "I'll see you later, ok?" Aurore let him out and he hurried down the dockyard, past the hulking Calpurnian frigates under repair. He looked back once, Aurore silhouetted dark against the light interior of *Golden Wanderer*, watching him.

CHAPTER
SEVEN

AURORE PUT her mug and Bel's in the cleaner. The ship was very quiet. But she wouldn't sleep until Dian was in. And now she had Bel's problems on her mind. She went instead to the command center. Nobody was there, the boards shut down, power at minimum. There was no reason for anyone to be here. *Golden Wanderer* was in berth for the final stage of refit.

She sat down in the captain's chair, caressing the soft leather arms of the couch, and leaned her head back.

She had been ten Days past her sixteenth birthday when she finished school. The next Greater Day, after everyone had recovered from the graduation party, she formally apprenticed to a House Melian merchant. Her grandfather kissed her goodbye before she went to the port offices to make her mark in the register. He wasn't up to going out anymore, but he reached his arms up from his bed and she put her head against his shoulder. "I am so proud of you," he whispered. "Just like my dad. Star-stuff in your blood." She hadn't cried. It was a day for joy.

Theo ran around on toddler feet trying to get into trouble. Dian was away at school. Her father beamed as the full port duty crew and the crew of the Melian merchanter Sun Dancer *applauded as she clicked every box in agreement to the terms.*

"You're part of the crew now," Captain Varnaros i Melian said, clapping her on the shoulder with a beefy hand. It wasn't possible to be any happier.

Twenty-eight hours later they jumped for Adelphi. The run up outsystem was fascinating. Aurore took the most junior seat, monitoring communications as they came up on the jump point.

"Strap in," the captain said. "Eleven minutes to jump."

She tilted her couch back, adjusting the neck pad correctly behind her neck. Neck injuries were the most common in jump, and there was a special pad to cradle the upper spine. She pulled the straps across, carefully fastening them on opposite sides of her body, shoulder to hip, the sternum pad held in the center. Her heart sped with excitement.

"Coming up on the jump point," the navigator said.

"Main engine burn in three, two, one..." Varnaros said.

The acceleration pushed her back, and then there was a sudden disconnection as Sun Dancer *leapt out of real space into the fold of the jump, three minutes and eleven seconds to cross lightyears.*

Silence. Sudden, complete silence. There was pressure, but it was like floating free, like the first moments she'd ever known of weightlessness, completely free of her body and her time. Aurore opened her mouth. For a moment there was nothing but quiet. And then she could hear them singing, the distant, perfect harmony of the stars. Streams of electrons flowed down the hull like warm currents at sea. They tumbled and played around Sun Dancer's *bow like leaping fish. Tendrils of rose and gold wreathed her. The universe danced with her.*

It was like plunging into the green waters off the coast of Beira, diving into the ocean with strong, young arms, carried on the breast of the sea. Each blurred sun sang back to her. The dark kissed her. She didn't understand the words. Not quite, like listening to a choir in a language half-known. And yet the music rose, carrying her upward. It lifted the ship, carried it like a rising crescendo through the Long Night.

And out. With a shiver, they reverted to real space. Pressure eased. Readouts stablilized, showing the normal coordinates of an intermediate jump point 20 lightyears from Menaechmi. Shipboard sounds returned.

"All systems normal," the first officer said.

"Twenty-one hours and eleven minutes until our next jump," the navigations officer said.

The captain looked at her. She had tears streaming down her face. "All right, Melian?"

"Yes, captain," Aurore said. She'd never been so all right in her life.

AURORE SMILED, remembering. It was like that every time, and in the nearly twelve years since then she'd learned that most people found jumps to be unpleasant if not painful. Dian didn't mind them, but that was as far as it went. Some people found them unbearably frightening, a sense of being pinned down with a weight on their chest for long minutes at a time. Crews avoided long jumps. Passengers often preferred some kind of sedation or anti-anxiety medication. She was the only person she knew who loved them. It was ecstasy.

Long jumps didn't bother her. Time seemed to stand still. It was moments or minutes of delight. She hated for them to end. She'd broached the subject with a senior medic who had a lot of experience with star crews.

The medic had shrugged. "Something about your personal neurological patterns," she said. "Jumps make some people sicker than others. You're lucky."

A quirk of neurology. She couldn't ask her grandfather if that was what he'd meant about his father. He died when she was seventeen.

Her family had fallen apart then, the secret of Merrow blood ripping apart her father's marriage, Mia born too soon because Lyra couldn't wait to get rid of her. Aurore had never liked Lyra anyway. "Natural jealousy of a twelve-year old toward a new stepmother," her father had said ponderously when she'd told him Lyra was a scorpion. She didn't refrain from saying she'd told him so five years later. Nobody listens to a twelve-year old about her stepmother, but sometimes the twelve-year old is right.

She'd taken a leave from *Sun Dancer* to take care of Theo while Mia was in the natal center. He was three years old and Dad couldn't be in two places at once. He was her baby brother and she loved him. When he put his little arms around her neck and begged her for stories of space, she told them gladly.

"...once in a hundred years, the Lord of the Dance calls to his lover," she said. "He sings to her from our shores, and she hears him out in the Long Night. Closer and closer, like a comet on a long orbit, she swoops in and he reaches for her, clouds building to the stratosphere. He brings the rain and she plunges to earth, lying together under the trees while the ocean sings back to them with tide of life. He draws her near and from them worlds are born."

"Everything is born," Theo said solemnly. "Everything. Even turtles."

"Even turtles," Aurore agreed. "Olive trees and orange trees. Cats and ruffled lizards. Fish and birds and you and me. Even the Golden Lady is born from them."

Theo sighed happily. "He's so lucky," he said.

"And then, when the time has come, she leaves again," Aurore said. "She goes back to the quiet beyond heliopause, Queen of Darkness. But she will always return to her lord."

"When he dances," Theo said.

"When he dances," Aurore agreed. She cuddled Theo close, but the tears in her eyes were for the beauty out there, the music of the Long Night.

As soon as it was possible, she returned to *Sun Dancer*.

At twenty-four she'd made captain fairly and honestly, first on the examination and with 99 out of 100 possible points from her sponsoring captain. Since then she'd run four different Melian ships, most lately *Golden Wanderer*. She'd begged her father to pull strings to get her a visitorship at the Morriganian War College, but he'd resisted. "What do you need war college for?" he'd said. "We don't have any warships."

We will, was on the tip of her tongue. But she wasn't Head of House yet and wouldn't be for a long time. And when she was, she'd be tied to Menaechmi as surely as if her feet had been nailed to the ground. She knew what the work of Head of House was. It was all-consuming. The responsibilities went from dawn of Greater Day to dark of Full Night. One could play hard, but leaving Menaechmi was out of the question. Hopefully her father would live to be ninety-two as her grandfather had. She didn't have to give it up. He wasn't yet sixty.

And so instead of War College she'd read everything she could find. She'd studied all the Morriganian tactical manuals she could. When they called on Morrigan she bought every memoir of the last Calpurnian War she could find. She even chatted up anyone from the Morriganian Fleet she met in bars in Heian Port or Holyrood. If anyone knew about war, it was the Morriganians. She didn't mind if people thought her an "armchair admiral." There was so much to know.

Aurore sat up, *Golden Wanderer*'s systems silent around her. Soon they'd dance the night again. Soon they'd go home, coming in-system like the Lady of the Void herself, drawn to the glittering band of light along the coast as Menaechmi turned. Coming home. And then putting out again. *Soon.* She caressed the control arm as though she whispered to an animal eager as she.

The courtesy chime pinged, and Aurore went to the hatch. Dian plunged through, her makeup blurred and her eyes red. "What happened?" Aurore demanded. "What did she do to you?"

"She didn't do anything. It's not like that." Dian pushed past her in the hall.

Aurore followed. "You're crying. What did she do?"

"Nothing." Dian shouted, turning at the entrance of the common room. "Victoria didn't do anything to me. She's going to die. That's all. Ok? Does that answer your question?"

"Why is she going to die?" Aurore asked. Dian could be a little high strung, but this seemed serious.

Dian went into the common room and plopped into the chair Bel had sat in, which Aurore took as tacit agreement to talk about it. "It's a long story."

"Well, I'll make you some coffee and you tell me," Aurore said. She was not going to get any sleep tonight, was she?

"Altissima Thurinia, the other faction leader, is coming to claim Lono," Dian said.

"I know that." Aurore worked the brewer. "Doesn't everybody know that?"

"Yes, we all know that." Dian put her head down on her arms. "Victoria isn't planning to surrender to her. She thinks Thurinia is terrible and she won't give her what's left of Iulus' fleet."

"That's good," Aurore said. "Because the Lonoi are planning to resist too. There's an heir to the Lonoi crown and he hates Thurinia too. So if Prince Belimar," she hesitated. It was strange to say. Aurore squared her shoulders. "If Prince Belimar can stop the Lonoi Resistance from attacking Antisia, they can make common cause against Thurinia."

Dian lifted her head, staring at Aurore incredulously. "The Lonoi Resistance?"

"Do you think you're the only one who's done anything while we were here?" Aurore said.

"The Lonoi Resistance?"

Aurore nodded cheerfully, handing Dian the mug of coffee. It was nice to not be the stick in the mud sometimes. "So I have contacts with the Lonoi Resistance and I know Prince Belimar. He'd rather make common cause with Antisia than fight her. So we broker that, they make a deal, and then they kick Thurinia's ass together." She sat down at the table. Dian stared at her. "Dad-levels of charm. We sort it all out."

Dian put her hands together around the mug, speaking very slowly and distinctly. "The problem is that Antisia doesn't have any ships. Or any troops. Or any missiles."

"What?"

"Her ships are crap. They were beat to pieces at Morrigan. She has one ship that's spaceworthy and battle worthy. She has one other ship which can actually move and isn't open to void. The other four are basically hulks in the Yards with months of work left on them. She has less than twenty missiles. Against Thurinia with six to ten battle-worthy ships and three hundred-plus missiles." Dian took a quick sip of her coffee, not even wincing at the heat. "She's dismissed her crews except for volunteers. I expect they're mostly people with families here. She's going to make a suicide stand. But it's not going to work and she knows it. Got it?"

Aurore blew out a long breath. "So if the Lonoi had an uprising now they'd meet almost no resistance. They'd just cut through everything and it would be a slaughter."

"Yes." Dian pushed her blue-tipped hair back with one hand. "They could just kill all the Calpurnians. Lono for Lono."

"That's not what Bel wants," Aurore said. "He doesn't want a slaughter."

Dian snorted. "Isn't that what people always want? Revenge? Do to them what they did to you?" She met Aurore's eyes. "Loose the Hounds of the Lord of the Dance? Does he seriously think he could stop them?"

"I don't know," Aurore said slowly. "He might." Belimar Calado, the Blameless Prince, might be able to if he had the Solaste Crown. There was almost an idea here.

"Besides," Dian said, "Even if he did prevent a slaughter and Victoria made a deal with him or something, there is still no fleet! One ship that's actually battleworthy. Five that aren't. No missiles. Unless your prince has a fleet stashed away somewhere, the only thing that would happen is that he'd get crushed too. Victoria thinks the battle is hopeless. She's just preparing to die with honor." Dian blinked hard.

The common room was quiet. There were the normal, peaceful sounds of *Golden Wanderer*'s rest, the ventilation system purring softly, the click of the food heater starting a self-cleaning cycle. Here, right this moment, was the fulcrum. Like so many times before, the two of them watching little Mia sleep with her monitors when she first came home, like sitting up on the roof together watching the dawn come, like they had as children, it was just the two of them. "It always comes down to us," Aurore said quietly. Stars and sea, the blazing nova and the rolling, golden dice, simple as coffee cups. She took Dian's hand across the table.

"We have to do something," Dian said. Her voice was hard. "I won't let her die."

"We won't let all of them die." Aurore shook her head. "It's not our world and not our fight and we're foreigners and have no right to interfere, but we're going to."

"I don't like tragedies and I'm not going to be in one."

"Bel needs to know there is no fleet," Aurore said. "He needs to know that Antisia has no ships to give him and that Thurinia is actually coming."

"Victoria needs to know that there's going to be a Rising." Dian said, lifting her head. "Or that there might be, if your prince can't make terms."

"He's got to make terms," Aurore said. "I don't know if he can. I don't think he's in charge."

"Then she's got to evacuate people." Dian shook her head. "How? There are tens of thousands of people with Calpurnian blood all over the planet. Even if you told them to leave everything they own…" Her voice trailed off.

"I'm going after Bel," Aurore said. "I know where he was going. You go to Antisia and warn her. Tell her Bel—Nereus Iulus—wants to make a deal. Let's deal with the Rising and then we'll deal with Thurinia."

Dian straightened up. She squeezed Aurore's hand and let it go. "Nutty bees."

"Nutty bees," Aurore said. She stood. "Let's do this."

THE SHRINE WAS dark except for the lantern over the door when Aurore's electric hired trundle pulled up. Fortunately, it was automated so it not only knew where she was going but didn't argue about doing it in the middle of the night. It just took her currency scan and left. Aurore rubbed her arms in her light jacket as she approached the door. It was cooler here than in Tranquility, the wind of the estuary feeling like winter instead of early spring. There was an elaborate pattern of stepping stones and a physical bell with a cord to pull. Aurore hesitated. There was no discreet way to do this, was there? Or maybe there was. She pulled out her handheld and pinged Bel. *At the entrance of the Shrine. Imperative to speak with you.*

She stood in the cold, looking down at the lights of Tranquility clear and bright. Above, lights in orbit showed where a capital ship was docked to tenders. Was that the spaceworthy one? She hadn't been able to tell on approach, though she certainly hadn't scanned it.

The door opened. Bel stood there in stockinged feet. "Aurore?" he said incredulously. "Why are you here?"

"I have to talk to you," she said. "Can I come in?"

"Sure." He stepped back. "Take your boots off before you come in the Shrine." Aurore took her boots off in the vestibule, a small space lit by a single lamp. "This way," Bel said.

He led her through a sliding door into a larger, square room, its polished floor surrounding a wooden statue in the center, the side toward her half charcoal, the Lord of the Dance with what might have been a drum in his hand. The black surface gleamed in the light from the vestibule. Aurore stopped in her tracks, bowing deeply. "Gracious Lord," she said. In the shifting light, his eyes seemed to fix upon her.

Bel was staring at her as she straightened up. "You're a worshipper?"

Aurore shook her head still looking at the statue. It waited, expressionless. "I'm not an initiate. But I've been to the Theon in Ancyra and seen His Bright Face." And that had been an experience to remember, though it had felt somehow incomplete, as though at twenty she had been incomplete, too young to more than touch on things still beyond her, a bird not yet fledged. She was not for his service, and not yet suited to some other. She bowed again. "Respect, my good lord."

"I see your friend understands," a voice said, and Aurore turned. The priestess stood in the doorway, her hair elaborately braided above her pale robe, though even in the dim light her voice sounded shaky. Tears? What deeply personal scene had Aurore interrupted. When she spoke again her voice was strong. "I am Sura."

"Captain Aurore Melian," she said, turning from the statue to the woman. "Bel, I've found out some things I need to tell you."

His eyebrows rose. "What's happened?"

"Altissima Thurinia is coming," Aurore said. "She'll have six or seven ships which are battleworthy. She's intending to crush Altissima Antisia and the Federationist faction. Thurinia is Social Logic. It wouldn't be like having Iulus as an overlord. It would be ten times worse. Antisia can't win the battle but she's planning to make a suicide run to see if she can take out Thurinia. Most likely it won't work. But if you attack Antisia now, you'll completely roll over her and hand Lono to Social Logic."

"Shit," Bel said. He looked at Sura. "Do you understand how bad that would be?" He paced around the statue, going to stand at the doors looking out into a cold garden. "I grew up in Adelphi and went to university on Calpurnia for a couple of years. Social Logic had a real following there. People were sick to death of the Politists and their policies. Going to the other extreme seemed attractive. Nuclear families instead of the good of the state. Mental health instead of collective action. All that stuff—but it was just as bad as the Politists when you scratched the surface. There was no room for individuality or expression. At the bottom, the philosophy was hollow."

"You sound like you entertained it," Sura said.

Bel looked at her inscrutably. "That's what kids do at university, right? Play with ideas. I played with Social Logic. Then I dropped out and joined the Lonoi Resistance."

"And then you left that." Sura drew herself up. "What do you really believe?"

"None of it," Bel said. "The Federationists are patrician oligarchs. The Politists are collectivist oligarchs. The Social Logic faction are extremist nuts. The Lonoi Resistance are nationalist dreamers. I'm not on any of these sides!"

"You've got to be something!" Sura snapped.

"Maybe I'm my own side," Bel said. "I can be that, can't I, Aurore? I'm Nereus Iulus. Belimar Calado. I can make my own side."

"Maybe you're a faction leader," Aurore said. "You can be."

Sura threw up her hands. "And what do you stand for?"

"Letting people make their own way under an umbrella of rules that keeps them from killing each other. Learning to live together in the world the way it is. The Innocent are here and Lono needs them. There are tens of thousands of people of mixed heritage who are just as Lonoi as the people whose ancestors didn't intermarry. Lono isn't one thing. It's a patchwork. And that's our strength—we're not all of a piece. Sometimes those pieces don't fit together nicely, but we can't just dye the whole cloth a single color and say it's one thing. It will still fall apart along every seam." Bel paced around the statue. "Right now everybody is going to be crushed by Thurinia. That's a good reason to make common cause. If I can get Antisia and the Resistance on the same side, maybe we can win."

Aurore winced. "That's the other thing I came to tell you. Antisia doesn't have a fleet."

"We can see it right there," Bel said, gesturing to the window.

"It's not battleworthy. In fact most of the ships aren't space worthy. She's dismissed her crews except for some who are willing to make a suicide stand, mostly because they have families on Lono. There is no fleet."

Sura put her hand to her face. "Surely not."

"It's 100 percent true. My sister had it from Antisia herself this evening." Aurore met her eyes firmly. "There are six ships and only one of them is capable of action, with one more that is space worthy but screwed up and four in the yards in pieces. Against six or seven of Thurinia's."

For a long moment both of them just stared at her. Then Bel looked at Sura. "And we've got Resistance leaders coming to talk to me in two hours. We are so screwed."

"Tell them the truth," Aurore said. "Surely their desire for self-preservation is stronger than their hatred for Altissima Antisia."

"Not so sure about that," Bel said with a twist of the lips. "I know Fayn and I've met Gurnie. There's a lot of sad songs about heroic last stands."

Sura closed her eyes. "I will not be the instrument of my world's destruction. I've fought against that fate all my life, Dark Lord. Please leash Your hounds."

"He can't," Aurore blurted. "That's not his job." Bel looked at her and she went on. "That's not the story. I've seen the Mysteries danced in Ancyra. She stays His hand, the Mother of Mercy, the Lady of the Void who is his lover. She sings to him from the depths of interstellar space and he listens. The hounds are lulled back to sleep by her song and leashed by her words."

"We do not call on her here," Sura said.

"Maybe you should start," Aurore said. "The Temple of the Lord of the Dance in Ancyra honors her as his consort."

"That's theology," Bel said. "And culturally interesting as it is, my problem is a big Calpurnian fleet looking for a war and a rebellion looking for revenge."

Sura let out a long breath, drawing herself up. "Then you'll need to meet the leaders with the full authority of the Calado Prince. You need to make the Descent."

"I don't have time for some…"

"You have to have the authority." For a moment Sura and Bel's eyes locked, but this time it was Bel who looked away.

"Fine," he said. "What do I do?"

"You asked before what was down there, below the Shrine. Now you will find out. You will go into the darkness with a companion and discover what there is to know. I will awaken a suitable acolyte."

Bel shook his head. "I pick my own companion. Aurore Melian." He looked at her. "If you'll go?"

"Yes," Aurore said. "I'm not an initiate, but I've been to the Mysteries." There was a prickling along her back, like the moments waiting on the tarmac before launch. Anticipation, but not fear. This wasn't dangerous, at least not for her.

For a moment Sura hesitated, then bowed her head. "So be it," she said.

ANTISIA WASN'T SLEEPING. After taking Dian back to the ship, her rooms had seemed very quiet, the rumpled bed a reminder of how empty it was. She could have asked Dian to stay the night, but she gathered that people from Menaechmi thought that sleeping in the same bed was offensive. Best not to end it on a sour note.

Antisia lifted her hand and poured herself another drink, fruit brandy on a minimum of ice. How many drinks was this? Too many. And not enough. How many drinks would it take for the future to stop rushing in, those moments inevitably to come on *Cornelia*? Would she go through with it? Or would her body betray her, shaking and irresolute? Would panic unman her at the last? With Dian here, she'd at least sounded like the person she wanted to be for a little while. Now there was nothing left. A few days. And then… Was there anything after, or just nonexistence? The old images she'd seen in mandatory cultural studies classes had showed those who died in space held to the breast of the Lady of the Void, but of course there was no such thing. Death was ceasing. Could she do it? Was pride strong enough?

The chime beside her bed rang. Antisia frowned. It was two hours until dawn. "Yes?" she replied.

The soldier sounded suitably apologetic. "Altissima, I regret to disturb you, but Dian Melian is here and says she must speak with you immediately. She's very insistent and refuses to leave. Should I arrest her?" *Unspoken, that she's a liaison of yours…*

"Send her up," Antisia said. Why was Dian back and making a scene? They'd said everything there was to say. She met her at the door.

Dian was still wearing the same clothes, though looking distinctly ruffled. She glared at the guard. "Your goon took forever to call you! Honestly, what a shit show!"

Antisia ushered her in and shut the door. "Why are you back?"

"Like I told that moron, I have something important to tell you." Dian tossed her hair back. "There's going to be a Rising."

"What?"

"A Rising." Dian took the glass out of Antisia's hand. "How much have you had to drink? Are you so scuppered you didn't understand what I said? A Rising. A Lonoi rebellion. Against you."

"What?" Antisia felt that she was several steps behind. "When?"

"Soon. Today. Tomorrow. The next few days." Dian tossed off what was left in the glass. "It's an even bet which will happen first—the Rising or Thurinia. Probably the Rising. In which case, the Rising plows you under and then Thurinia shows up and boldly retakes Lono. So the Rising slaughters the Calpurnians and the Innocent, and then Thurinia slaughters the rebels. She wins. She sweeps the board. Big hero on Calpurnia. She's Autarch."

Antisia closed her eyes. "Of course," she said. Her chest hurt for some reason.

"I'm guessing you don't have the troops to put down a Rising."

"No," Antisia said. "But I'll have to, won't I? If we're attacked by the Lonoi rebels, we have to defend ourselves. Evacuation is impossible. Tens of thousands of people…"

"What if you didn't have to?" Dian asked. Antisia opened her eyes. Dian quirked one eyebrow. "I said, what if you didn't have to? What if you could come to an agreement with the Calado Prince?"

"The Calado Prince? The last Calado Prince died decades ago. Also, why would he do that?" Antisia shook her head. "How could I do that?"

Dian looked like a gambler with an ace in the hole. "Because he's Nereus Iulus. Belimar Calado and Nereus Iulus are the same person. He gave you the documents. His mother is Amari Calado. The Calado Prince and the Autarch's heir are the same."

"I don't..." She'd advised him to run. She hadn't considered his mother, not even looked up her identity. Why would she? His father was the important thing, the Calpurnian parent, the man she knew.

"You may not be able to make terms with the Calado Prince, but you can with Nereus Iulus. You can make a deal. He wants a deal. He's half Calpurnian. He doesn't want to kill all the Calpurnians. And he hates Social Logic and doesn't want Thurinia to win." Dian poured more brandy into the glass.

"Nereus Iulus and the Calado Prince are the same person?" Antisia felt like she was still running about two steps behind.

"And don't you know the Autarch planned it this way?" Dian said. "I've never heard he was a careless man. Do you think he just happened to have a child with the Calado heir to the throne? By accident? Don't you think he hoped to get an heir who could rule, just like the Warlord Khreesos before him? That's the story, right? Khreesos got a daughter on the Calado Princess who claimed all Lono and established a dynasty. When he had those documents made thirty years ago, don't you think he knew what he was doing?"

Antisia took a deep breath. They'd stood on the balcony outside his office, Iulus's profile sharp against the twilight lights on the mountain behind, streets slick with rain below them, the clouds blowing out to sea. A son, he'd said. Nereus Iulus. A boy he hadn't seen since babyhood. There had been a wistful sound in his voice. His only child, fathered long ago with a woman he didn't name, a reminder of the young man he'd been, foolish and idealistic who hadn't yet become all he was. He'd told her. She'd wondered why. Perhaps he just wanted to tell someone. Or perhaps he wanted her to know just in case.

Antisia blinked. Just in case he was killed. As had happened. He had been assassinated on Calpurnia while she struggled to get her ships into Lono. She had made no funeral oration for him. She had not brought his assassins to justice. And yet the hounds of the Lord of the Dance had run them down, House Melian the instrument of their destruction. And Dian Melian had brought this to her.

"He didn't tell you?" Dian asked gently.

"He told me he had a son, Nereus Iulus. He didn't tell me who the boy's mother was." Antisia shook her head. "I didn't ask."

"It wasn't important, was it?"

"No." She reached for the glass, but Dian held it away, smiling.

"You've had enough," Dian said. "You've got to sober up to meet with the Calado Prince. Maybe there doesn't have to be a Rising."

Antisia lifted her head. "Did he plan it that way? Or did he just hope?"

"Hope is a powerful thing." She heard the click of the ice as Dian took another drink. "Maybe this Nereus Iulus is the thing you've been looking for."

"You put a lot of faith in crowns and bloodlines."

"I put a lot of faith in family," Dian said.

He had been a father to her, or what Dian called a father. And he had given her a secret. She had been the one who had everything Nereus Iulus had not—his love and attention, his pride and his confidence—while his son had always wondered. And now it was on them, the two of them, the mismatched Autarch's heirs, the child of his body and the child of his heart.

"We'll make a deal," she said. "Can you find him? I don't know where he is."

"He's with my sister," Dian said. "Leave it to me."

CHAPTER
EIGHT

THE STEPS LED DOWN into the dark. Sura had pulled the curtain aside, and Bel stood at the top, looking down at the stairs. Behind him, Aurore held an old-fashioned candle in a glass lamp.

"Seriously?" Bel said. His tone sounded a little hollow even to him. He'd been terrified of these steps as a child, terrified and fascinated at once. He remembered that. An acolyte had pulled him back from the brink, telling him it was not for him. It was. But not when he was three.

"It's ok," Aurore said. She looked comfortingly sane, a merchant captain in her work clothes, nothing spooky or weird about her.

"What's down there?" Bel asked. "Do you even know?"

For a moment the mask seemed to slip. "I know," Sura said, "but I renounced it long ago."

"You are the Calado Princess," Bel said. "Why didn't you claim it?"

"You, of all people, ask that?" Sura touched his chest with one hand, the only time she'd touched him.

"You married him in secret," Bel said. "Sanius Iulus. You wouldn't lead a rebellion against your husband. Not in all these years when he was Viceroy."

"Nor did he crush us," Sura said. "And he could have." She looked away. "We had hoped—foolishly, I suppose, when we were very young

—that we could make things different. But that could not happen. He was assassinated by Calpurnians, not by us, though I gather some plotted at it."

They'd met in a cellar smelling of salt water beneath one of the warehouses along the estuary. The foundation was old. It had been something before the Calpurnians came.

Fayn was there, and Porrie and Ustad and one more. Fayn had laid it out. Bel could pass as a wealthy Calpurnian visitor, the kind of man who might request a private audience with the Autarch. "We can do this," Fayn said, taking a drink from a tea flask. "We can kill the Viceroy. We can retake Lono."

Bel shook his head. "Assassinate Altissimus Iulus? That's crazy. There are guards. There are electronic systems. There are weapons detectors. I'll give you that I could get into the Viceregal Palace. I could maybe even come up with a story that would get me an audience with him. But not carrying a weapon. They're not stupid. I can't walk in there with an energy flail or a big knife, take out a couple of guards who are probably armed, and then kill him!"

"A private audience," Fayn said. "You can make that happen. Tell him you have something important. Some information so sensitive you need to say it privately. That will get you into the office without guards."

Bel spread his hands. "Maybe."

Fayn leaned forward. "There is nothing that will stop one man's hands alone in a private room, an old man and a young man who is willing to die for a cause. You get close. And then you do it."

He could see how. He could imagine the Viceroy sitting at his desk, looking up something on the screen at Bel's direction. He'd cross behind him. And then the arm around the throat, the choking move that cut off air and prevented a cry for help. He was strong. He'd have his weight. Against an old man sitting down…

"I won't do it," Bel said clearly.

"Because you wouldn't get out alive?" Porrie asked.

"This is bigger than one man," Fayn said. "Assassinating the Viceroy is worth a life. You'd be honored forever. No, you wouldn't get out. But you'd have done something that lasts forever. You'd have freed Lono."

Bel could almost feel the man's throat in his hands, feel his weakening, erratic pulse. "I won't do it. I'm not an assassin."

"What you are is a coward," Porrie said.

To kill like that, coldly and ruthlessly… "I'm out," Bel said. He stood up. "Find somebody else."

He had come that close. He could have stood in that office beside the Solaste Crown, met his father and killed him. Of course he'd have gotten the private audience if he'd given his name. Of course Iulus would have turned his back on him, his son become the instrument of his destruction. That was an old story, the parricide who brings down every curse.

Instead, he'd walked away. He'd left Lono. He wasn't an assassin.

Someone else was. The Politist faction leaders had. Cassian and Junia had assassinated Sanius Iulus and been killed in turn, one more twist in this endless, deadly game.

Aurore touched his elbow. "Let's do this," she said gently. "There's nothing down there you can't handle."

She was right. He'd already met the monsters. "Let's go." Bel stepped down into the dark.

The stairs turned after one flight, no lights along them lit. There was a rail. There was Aurore's lamp. The light above was quenched by Sura dropping the curtain and closing the door. They went down. One flight, two, then three. They must be below the basement level of the Shrine. At the fourth flight the walls were rough, organic, the steps cut into rock.

"A cave?" Aurore guessed.

"It's a big bluff over the estuary," Bel said. "Probably old watercourses. Older than the Shrine. Maybe older than Tranquility." His words ran ahead of him, down into the dark, and he shivered. It was cold.

Aurore lifted the lamp so they could see better. "What's supposed to be here?"

"I don't really know," Bel said. "It's a ritual. I'd guess it has something to do with the Phoenix of the Sun." He stopped, glancing back at her. "It's some kind of mythical creature that comes when the right Prince or Princess calls it and did for about five hundred years. I don't see how something like that could exist."

"Legends usually have some basis in fact," Aurore said thoughtfully but not entirely helpfully.

"I hope not," Bel said. "The last thing we need is a monster. We've got enough problems."

"I've never understood how giant monsters are supposed to live in caves," Aurore said, following him. "What do they eat?"

"No idea," Bel said. Below, the stair opened out, and he hesitated. He could feel the movement of air on his face like a much larger space was ahead. Aurore lifted the lamp higher.

It was a cave, perhaps part of a much larger network, the ceiling higher than the small light would penetrate. The floor had been smoothed somewhat, and ahead lay three large shapes shrouded in black cloth. Each was perhaps three meters long and a meter wide, lying side by side in the darkness.

"A tomb?" Aurore guessed.

"Graveyard of the Calado Princes?" Bel stepped forward, and they crossed the floor to the first shape. His voice echoed even though he spoke softly. He steeled himself for the sight of some sort of twisted mummified remains and lifted the first cloth.

Gold glittered suddenly bright, but it wasn't jewels about the neck of a corpse. There were no bodies here, no sarcophagi. He drew the cloth back and it dropped to the ground with a susurrating sound. Folded golden wings cast back the light, held tight against a long metal body, red and bronze, poised on landing gear like claws.

"Some sort of drone?" Aurore said. "With retractable wings for atmospheric flight?"

"Who builds something like that?" Bel said. He ran his hand over the wing, the thin solar cloth soft under his fingers.

"Those look like old Morriganian solar cells," she said. "They use solar to power their orbital stations. They're not geostationary. When they go around the light side of Morrigan they recharge. I've taken merchanters into Orbital Three and Orbital Four. That's what the solar arrays look like. Only these are much, much smaller. But why would Morriganian drones be here?"

"The Warlord Khreesos," Bel said. It all fit together. "Khreesos and his fleet were the first to rediscover Lono after the Lost Times. Lono didn't have any sophisticated technology. He had a child with the Calado Princess and gave her a crown for the baby. And he probably left these drones as a means of protection. After all, they were far more sophisticated than anything on Lono then."

Aurore raised the light again. "It looks like there are two more launchers here which are empty."

"The Phoenix of the Sun," Bel said. Not a monster. Not a religious experience. Of course. "That's what they are. Twice in the first fifty years the Phoenix attacked the Princess's enemies with fire. And then later the Phoenix was seen but didn't attack. She used two of the five drones. Then the others were just flown to make a ceremonial appearance. The last time was two hundred and eighty years ago."

Aurore walked around the nose of the drone they'd uncovered, trailing her hand along the surface. "They're beautiful. And they look like they're in great shape."

"Which is super if I want to fly them and claim supreme monarchy," Bel said, "but I don't. Let's start with that I think monarchy is a terrible governmental system. I don't think there should be a Blameless Prince and a restored traditional monarchy! Not me, not anybody else. Before the Just War, Calpurnia had a democracy. It wasn't perfect, but at least there was representation, not just absolute rulers who could do whatever they pleased. The last Calado Princes were bad rulers. Even Sura says so. People may sing today about how great the lost princes were, but it's just sentiment. Mystery of the Phoenix of the Sun solved, but it doesn't get us anywhere."

"I wonder if we could use them against Thurinia," Aurore mused.

"Even if they have some kind of weaponry, three atmospheric drones against a Calpurnian battle fleet? They're smaller than a 250 missile."

"Yeah, I'm not seeing it," Aurore said. "I'm sure they were really scary against ground infantry with swords back in the day, but that was a long time ago." She turned, sweeping the light around as much as she could. It didn't penetrate far. "There's probably a control board around here somewhere. We could hunt for it if you want to fly them."

"Not a big priority," Bel said. He looked around the cavern. It wasn't a mysterious labyrinth. It was just a basement that drones were stored in. For some reason he felt oddly hollow. It wasn't like he'd expected some profound experience. He had a job to do and it was only getting later. "So let's get back upstairs and talk to Fayn and Gurnie. That's going to be hard enough without getting the Phoenix of the Sun into the conversation."

"You know I'll help however I can," Aurore said.

Bel looked at her, a slender figure in black holding the lamp aloft. "Why? This isn't your world."

"Because I'm here and I can."

After a moment, he held out his hand and she clasped it wrist to wrist. "Good enough," Bel said.

FAYN LOOKED the same as he always had, a nondescript man with a day's beard in nondescript working man's clothes. You could pass him a dozen times in the street and never notice him. Gernie was tall and angular, no older than Bel though his face was scarred with the pockmarks of childhood disease. He must have grown up on one of outer islands that didn't vaccinate, Bel thought, or among Iconoclasts who didn't believe in it.

They came through the Shrine's kitchens with one of the acolytes, Gernie's hands in his pockets. Bel made note of that. Probably a shell knife that wouldn't show on any metal scanners.

Fayn made a respectful bow to Sura, his smile fading as he looked up and recognized Bel. "Bel Alan."

"Actually, it's Belimar Calado," Bel said. He made himself smile as Fayn blinked. "Come on, Fayn. You didn't think Bel Alan was my real name, did you?"

"What kind of game is this?" Gernie asked.

"I assure you, it's no game," Sura said. "This is Belimar Calado, a Descendant of the Sun and claimant to the Solaste Crown. I would be happy to show you the proof. And I'm sure in due course of time he will be happy to call the Phoenix of the Sun, thus proving his legitimate right."

Aurore's eyes widened slightly, but that was all. She had a good face for a gamester.

Fayn looked at him sharply. "You think you're going to lead the Rising? After walking out on us?"

"No, I think you're going to call off the Rising," Bel said smoothly. "After you've heard what I have to say."

"Why would we do that?" Gernie said. "Unless you've already betrayed us to the Calpurnians."

"Because if Lono rises now, it will play into the hands of the Social Logic faction and deliver us all to the most oppressive regime you can imagine, one that will make the previous government look like benefactors. I'd like to stop that."

"Altissima Thurinia is coming," Aurore said. "If you've done her the favor of taking out Antisia, she'll just walk in."

"Who is she?" Fayn asked.

"Aurore Melian, Captain of the Menaechman merchanter *Golden Wanderer*," Aurore said. "So I don't have a dog in this fight. I warned Bel because I don't want to see that happen. And I'm no friend of the Calpurnians. Cassian and Junia tried to shake down my family. Now they're dead."

"Why should we trust you? You walked out on us." Fayn looked at Bel.

"And I didn't turn you over to the authorities, did I?" Bel asked. He shrugged. "I could have. Instead I walked away from your crazy scheme. Now I'm trying to talk you out of this one before you make things worse."

Gernie shook his head. "And you're claiming to be the Calado Prince?"

"He is the Calado Prince," Sura said.

"Why are you so sure?" Gernie responded. "He's a con man."

"He's my son," Sura said. There was steel in her voice. "And you know exactly who I am. So let's sit down and talk because we don't have much time."

Aurore's comm bracelet gave a discreet ping, the sequence Dian's code, and she slipped away from the discussion, through the hanging curtain into the shrine proper. It was entirely dark except for the light coming in through the many-paned doors, and the Effigy's eyes seemed to follow her as she padded through the room and opened the doors to the garden, sliding out and shutting them behind her. She activated the comm. "What's the story?"

"Where have you been?" Dian demanded. "I've been pinging you for more than an hour! I was about to take drastic action!"

"Sorry, I've been in the basement and didn't have a signal," Aurore said.

"The fuck."

"I'm sorry," Aurore said more loudly. "I was busy. I had a job to do too. So what happened? Did you talk to the Altissima?"

"Yes, she's right here. She's willing to deal with Nereus Iulus."

Aurore let out a deep breath. She sat down on the stone wall, looking out over the estuary at the lights of Tranquility on the other side. The dawn was coming, a rose tint to the sky far gentler than Menaechmi's thunderous sunrises. "Excellent."

"I thought you'd say so. So what about your guy?"

Aurore glanced back toward the doors. "He's meeting with some people right now. He's willing to deal but he's got to get his people to the table first so he has the authority to negotiate."

"That's all honey," Dian said. "She can deal with Nereus Iulus. If you can get him to the table, we'll get a deal."

"I can get him to the table," Aurore said. She stretched her cramped legs out. It had been a long night. "He's got to talk these people around but I think he can. The Shrine is backing him."

There was an indistinct voice behind, probably the Altissima listening to this. "He's not leaving planet," Dian said to her, "He's here." And then to Aurore, "Do you have any idea how long you'll be?"

"No idea," Aurore said. "Should we come to the Viceregal Palace when we're ready?"

"That's a plan," Dian said, and signed off.

Aurore shook her head. Maybe she should go back into the shrine where the discussion was happening, but maybe not. Bel had to do this. Her mental voice sounded a lot like her father, saying cynically that if Bel couldn't handle his own people, he wouldn't be able to bring any of this off. If he wasn't capable, best to find out now before the stakes got any higher. She took a deep breath, wishing she had coffee.

The last cup was wearing off and it had been a long night. Still, it was peaceful here, the cherry tree beginning to lose its blossoms like pale pink snow in the dawn breeze off the estuary. Gentle. This shrine was tranquil. Nothing about the Lord of the Dance was tranquil on Menaechmi.

She had gone to the Theon when she was twenty, a gift for her milestone birthday, and one greatly envied by the crew of the merchanter she served on. A night with an Adept was a dream for many, something to be saved for many years, but her father had been given it as a gift for his twentieth birthday, and now he gave it to her. Aurore welcomed it. It was a chance to explore some of the darker things she'd never dared to do with friends, too cautious to put her raw desires in the hands of people she liked but didn't love. An Adept was different. He wouldn't judge her, and in all likelihood she would never see him again. If she did it would be years from now in a completely different context, not tomorrow afternoon at a pickup game of wildball with half her relatives there.

The senior Adept who interviewed her was older than her father, a disson with understanding eyes. "Not much older than me," Aurore said. "Xalepos. Handsome. Kind." She paused. "Submissive." His expression didn't change. "And for the pavilion, Palatial. A palace fit for a queen and her humble courtiers."

His name was Adrian, and he was everything she'd hoped, green-eyed, gentle, begging her to deem him worthy. He'd controlled the scene subtly, letting her explore and discover her tastes while professing that he was entirely at her service. Afterwards, she'd lain on purple silk sheets while he massaged her legs, her head pillowed on her arms. "Did you always want to be an Adept?" she asked.

There was a smile in his voice. "I trained as a professional dancer from the time I was ten. But at twenty I realized that I wanted more than to be in a chorus, so I auditioned here. That was three years ago. It's a different life, but it's the right one for me right now."

She closed her eyes. "So you might not stay?"

"Most Adepts don't stay forever. A few, like Apollodorus who interviewed you, root to the floor and stay here until they kick it, but for most it's ten or fifteen years. Then you retire and do something else."

It was an amazing thing, to simply remake oneself when one wished. "What will you do then?"

His hands didn't falter, kneading her calves. "I don't know yet. I'll find out when the time comes. And you? What do you want to do?"

It didn't seem absurd to say it to him. "I want to lead a battlefleet."

Adrian started working just at the back of her knee. "Ambitious."

"Ridiculous," Aurore said, "when Menaechmi has no fleet. House Melian won't even arm our merchanters with bow chasers. But I could do it. I know I could with the right training. I could be good. I'm no worse than the Calpurnians and Morriganians my age who are learning on ships of the line. But I'm House Melian's heir. I can't run away and be a pirate or something. And I'm lucky. I work on a good ship and I'm learning how to command a merchanter. That's something."

"That's quite a lot, actually," Adrian said. "Who do you worship?"

"The Golden Lady," she replied. "All my family does."

Now his hands did pause. "Not the Lady of the Void? A lot of star travelers do."

"I don't really know her worship," Aurore said.

"We worship her as consort to her lover, the Lord of the Dance." Adrian spread more oil on his hands. "That's our sacred marriage. She…" He hesitated, looking for the right words. "…moderates him. He can be excessive, whether in ecstasy or as the avenger. She tempers him, brings him back from madness. He needs her to prevent him from going too far. That's always the problem, right? A little wine makes you happy and too much makes you sick. A reasonable amount of anger helps you focus and achieve and too much makes you a dangerous crank. She quenches fires."

"That makes sense," Aurore said. Certainly nothing quenched fire like void. Deprive it of oxygen and it went out in an instant. Cool. Peaceful. Not empty, but quiet. Menaechmi was never quiet. Everything brimmed with life.

"Sometimes even the gods need to rest," Adrian said.

THE SUN WAS RISING over Tranquility, but the light did not yet touch the courtyards of the Viceregal Palace. Antisia took another sip of her scalding coffee. Her head was throbbing, the topical hangover medication not quite absorbed and working yet.

"Is there any honey?" Dian asked, looking at the coffee service with exasperation, her cup in her hand. "Who serves coffee without honey?"

"It's not usual on Calpurnia," Antisia said, "but I can call for some if you like."

"Please," Dian said. She still looked terrific despite having been up all night and wearing the same clothes she'd been wearing yesterday. Her blue-tipped hair was only a little mussed.

Before she could open the intercom, it buzzed for her. "Altissima, your party has arrived. Nereus Iulus, the Keeper of the Shrine, and Captain Aurore Melian."

"I'll see them in the Autarch's office," Antisia said.

Dian smiled. "Show time."

"I have no idea what that means."

"You have no shows." Dian held onto her cup. "Ugh. Black coffee is better than none. Though I'd swear you bought this from Caserta, not Beira. It's bitter. It wasn't grown at altitude."

"I wouldn't know," Antisia said bemusedly, letting Dian precede her out of the room.

"I would," Dian said. "It's my job to identify broad provenance from taste. Coffee and wine and oil are easy. Oranges are hard."

"You actually know your work," Antisia said as she went down the stairs.

"Surprise!" Dian said. "Really, truly a merchant princess. I may be a wastrel, but I'm not completely ignorant of the business."

Nereus Iulus was waiting in the antechamber to the office, two security guards and one of the clerks waiting with him. Behind him, the priestess waited serenely, her hands in her trailing ornate sleeves, while Captain Melian looked around the room with a curious gaze, taking everything in. "A pleasure, Altissima," he said, with a slight and very correct bow.

"And for me," she said with an identical correct bow. "Shall we go in?"

"As you wish," he said, preceding her with his party. Antisia stopped the others at the door with the exception of Dian, ignoring the security guards' worried looks. This was not going to be a fight.

The door closed behind them. They stood in Iulus' office, the dim ambient lights coming on at their movements, the desk quiet and still, nothing on its smooth surface. In its case, the Solaste Crown glittered on its stand. He was not here. Antisia knew that. And yet for a moment she thought she caught a whiff of scent, a breath of something that was Iulus.

"Altissima, we have a problem," Nereus said. He looked alert, grave, trustworthy. Or at least he was trying to be.

"We?"

"You and I, since I am the Autarch's heir and what happens on Lono concerns me as well. There is a Rising planned, and we know that there are not the troops to put it down and to deal with Thurinia. I believe we are of the same mind that Social Logic's triumph would be a bad thing, not just for Lono but for Calpurnia itself. Fortunately, with the aid of Sura, the priestess of the Shrine, I have opened talks with leaders of the Rising and they are willing to come to terms."

Antisia let out a deep breath. "And what would those terms be?"

"Lonoi independence from Calpurnia is the goal," Nereus said.

"You know I can't do that." Antisia's voice was even. "That's a decision of the Senate, not one person, even if I were Autarch."

"We understand that," the priestess said.

"Of course you can't," Nereus said. "But what you can do is make me—Belimar Calado, Nereus Iulus—Viceroy of Lono. As the Viceroy, you can appoint your successor to the office. Nereus Iulus is an Altissimus, the son of the Autarch, and can legally serve."

"And Belimar Calado is the heir of the Calado princes," the priestess said, "And thus acceptable to the Lonoi people."

Was this what Iulus had planned all along? Or simply a wild chance that had appeared? "And what is to happen to me?" Antisia asked evenly.

"You are the commander of the Calpurnian troops present in the Lono system, the Altissima commanding six starships," Nereus said. "With which you will resist Thurinia as you had planned."

And die as she had planned. Antisia took a long breath. Yet it was the best plan. It would safeguard the families of her crews still on Lono, as well as all the Calpurnians who simply lived here. Nereus—

Bel Alan—or whoever he was, wasn't going to allow a massacre. If she could take out Thurinia in a suicide attack, they might all have a chance.

His eyes were solemn. "I give you my word that I will guard our people. All of them."

"You know that if Thurinia wins, that may not be possible." Out of the corner of her eye she saw Dian move slightly, though she said nothing.

"It may not be," Nereus said. "But I'll do my best. And I know you will. Maybe, between us, we can do this."

"Then we have an agreement," Antisia said. It felt like laying something down she had carried too long.

He reached for her hand, clasping it wrist to wrist. "We do. And we will make this work."

THE ALTISSIMA WENT BACK into the outer office to draw up paperwork, Sura following with Bel's handheld and the downloaded proofs of who he was—good fakes, Bel had thought. Now he knew the documents were real, kept by his mother all these years. No, not his mother. Sura. His mother was the woman who had raised him in the Adelphi Rim. What was he going to tell her about all this? Well, nothing if Altissima Antisia didn't win. But if she did, even if Antisia ended up dead, he could get his life back. Viceroy was an office. He could resign in favor of the right person, or maybe even make it an elected office. It was just a role he was playing for now. He'd do it well and get Thurinia off their backs and then see where they were.

Aurore and her sister were talking in furious whispers, and then her sister followed the others out. Aurore walked over to the Solaste Crown, her fingers trailing along the outside of the glass. "It's beautiful."

"It is," he said, seizing on the distraction. "I was hired to steal it." That seemed about a year ago, not a few days.

"And now it's yours." Aurore looked up at him, a little smile on her face. "Personal property of Sanius Iulus, and now of his son."

"I suppose it is." It hung there on the black velvet pedestal, long chains of gold glimmering in the case lights, looping around a heavier forehead band and crossing the top of the head in intricate patterns. There was something seductive about it, as though it hummed with music too low to hear.

"Do you want to try it on?" Aurore glanced at him sideways. "It's not claiming the crown," Aurore said. "It's just trying it on."

"I don't believe in absolute monarchs," Bel said. And yet the crown had an allure in itself, not in what it symbolized. His fingers itched for it. Was that how Iulus had felt, that grim and clever man he'd never met? What had it meant to him truly? Power, or an imaginary world in which he ruled with Sura beside him, little Bel posed in front of them like the stiff, overdressed children in historic images? Or was it the desire to touch the legacy of the Warlord Khreesos? He'd never know.

Aurore said nothing, just shrugged.

Bel slid his hand around the lower rim of the case, expertly finding the hidden catch. Press and turn. The case opened. Small, thin wafers of gold shimmered in the sudden breeze. "How does it…ah." Bel lifted it gently off the black velvet stand. The golden petals were affixed to a band beneath, a base metal cool under his fingers, titanium perhaps. And why not? The Morriganians had been technologically developed even in Khreesos' era.

"He gave it to Princess Lutece, his love, to keep for their daughter," Bel said. Each perfect leaf, each perfect petal, was crafted of ruddy gold. And yet where his fingers touched the band, it was cold.

"It's amazing," Aurore said. "Beautiful beyond belief." She smiled. "Can't hurt to try it."

"I suppose not." He wanted her to urge him. And yet the desire to put it on was his. Bel raised it carefully, the hanging garlands brushing against his shoulders, and set it on his head. There was a whisper of gold, and then the cold metal band beneath touched his temples.

The world expanded. For a moment there was a suffusion of golden light, as though he stood at the center of a brightly lit stage, people moving in the darkness all around him, quiet conversations and shuffling movements, and then cool dark. Comfortable. Safe. A reset had tripped, something returning to center, adapting to him.

A wearable interface, Bel thought. He'd never seen one, but he'd heard of them: a Morriganian Greater Gift, an interface attuned to some particular genetic profile.

Cool. Dark. He was in the cave beneath the Shrine, looking at the drones in their cradles, outside and inside them at once, looking up at him from their sensors. And there was the feedback, local memory supplying the most recent data, soaring like a gilded dragonfly above the streets of Tranquility, over the heads of the cheering crowd before the Viceregal Palace... Only it wasn't as he knew it, older, windows unblocked, the estuary free of its usual smog... The Phoenix of the Sun hadn't been seen in two hundred and eighty years. He was the Phoenix. He soared and dived, looping in the bright air, lifted on the wings of their paen just as he was on the unfurled solar wings of the drone. Phoenix of the Sun.

Three drones waited. They lay in their cradles beneath the Shrine, waiting for his word. If he willed it, they would rise, lifting from their cradles and owning the skies. They wanted to. They shivered, waiting for his hand.

Bel took a deep breath. He opened his eyes. Yes, he could see. He was standing in the office, Aurore looking at him with a concerned expression. He could be here and now. They would wait. He could speak.

"Are you all right?" Aurore asked.

"It's a control system for the drones," Bel said. He could push it down easily enough, the interface quiescent. "It's some kind of fly by wire system. The Solaste Crown controls the drones through a wearable interface. The Warlord Khreesos gave Princess Lutece a Greater Gift that could only be used by someone with the right genetic profile, assuring that the line couldn't be usurped. If the Calado Prince or Princess had to prove their right to the Crown by making the Phoenix of the Sun appear, it had to be a descendant of his."

"And just incidentally the drones were armed," Aurore said. "So that Lutece and their daughter had an impressive technologically superior weapon at their disposal. That makes so much sense."

"I can use the interface," Bel said. A thought occurred. "I bet Sura can too."

"But she won't," Aurore said.

Bel let out a deep breath. "So if I need to prove I'm the real deal, I can. I can make the Phoenix of the Sun appear. I could fly one of the drones over a crowd of skeptics."

"Good to know," Aurore said.

"I should put this back in the case." It was comfortable. It wanted him to wear it. It wanted him to be the Blameless Prince. And yet he wasn't trying to claim absolute monarchy. Bel reached up and lifted it off his head.

Aurore helped him put it back on the stand, arranging the strands carefully. "If you need it."

"If I need the authority, I can get it," Bel said. He closed the case again. "But I'm trying not to. And while it's beautiful and an amazing artefact, it doesn't solve any of our problems."

"Unfortunately," Aurore agreed.

Bel squared his shoulders. "The next step is figuring out if there's any way to get more of Antisia's ships functional. Maybe I can shake some of the fitters loose and get them to get a move on."

"I expect she's thought of that," Aurore said.

"Worth a try." Bel gestured to the door. "Coming?"

"Of course," Aurore said.

SOMEONE HAD FINALLY REMEMBERED to bring a breakfast cart, Aurore thought, filling her plate in the conference room. She'd been up all night and food was welcome. The conference room was an odd hybrid like everything else here, with walls covered in antique woven cloth pads and a shiny black conference table that could multiscreen or be one giant single screen as requested.

Tenn Mari joined her, a cup of tea in his hand. "Captain Melian," he said with relief in his voice. "So you're in on whatever this is?"

"Yes," Aurore said. "You told me how bad it would be if Thurinia and Social Logic took over Lono. So how do we stop that happening?"

"Does Nereus Iulus have a fleet up his sleeve?" Tenn asked.

At that point Antisia called the meeting to order, everyone settling down around the conference table except the aides taking notes and Dian, who lurked in the back with them, a world-weary expression on her face. Actually, she was probably just tired. Aurore sat at the table between Bel and the fitters. There were five of them besides Tenn, representatives of the largest Innocent firms in Tranquility, and every single one of them looked nervous or skeptical. She couldn't blame them. Antisia introduced Bel and then he made an impassioned plea for the fitters to redouble their efforts.

Aurore shook her head inwardly. She'd seen her father move many a meeting, and this one wasn't budging. She watched their body language, arms close to the body, shoulders over their hips, heads below the midline. Bel was getting nowhere. When he wound up, there was silence.

At last Tenn Mari glanced up and down his side of the table. "Altissimus, with all due respect, none of that makes any difference. It's not a question of whether we want to refit the ships. It's not a question of our effort. The truth is that two of them are beyond repair and two others cannot be made space worthy with the material we have." He held up a hand to forestall argument. "By that I mean that it is not possible to render them capable of holding atmosphere. There are thousands of micropittings. There are cracks and structural damage. There are compromised hull panels that are not sound. If we had two years and infinite material, we could strip them down to the bulkheads and completely rebuild the outer hulls. But we do not have enough plating to come anywhere close to replacing 100 percent of the exteriors, and doing so would require thousands of hours of labor in zero-g and suits because they are currently impossible to land in atmosphere due to the same hull compromises. If you tried to bring them into the yards, they'd implode on approach from atmospheric pressure. This cannot be done."

One of the other fitters nodded. "Altissimus, four of the six ships are beyond repair. They cannot be made functional for crews. No air, no water reclamation… I'm not talking about the tanks. We can replace tanks. What we can't easily replace is the thousands of meters of line that provides water throughout the ship. There are breaks and tears everywhere. And it's the same with the atmospherics. Sure, I can put in tanks. But with so many breaches, you're going to bleed out in void in a matter of minutes, not hours."

Antisia winced. Probably nobody but Aurore noticed because they were looking at Bel. Well, except Dian.

"Altissimus, you've got to accept this," Tenn said. "This can't be done. There is no way to put crews on those ships."

"There are two ships," Bel began.

"Yes, Altissimus," the other fitter said. "There are two which are under repair, *Cornelia* in orbit and *Determination* in the yards, one a ship of the line and one a frigate. It is possible for them to be made spaceworthy, though between them there are only twenty-five missiles, and *Cornelia* only has one functioning launcher. That's with reduced crews and far from optimal maneuvering. I wouldn't try to go to jump in either one. The hull stresses could be deadly."

"But in the system, in relatively straightforward flight?" Bel asked.

Tenn shrugged. "They'd hold up for a while. You could fight them if you didn't expect much."

"Two ships," Bel said, seeking Antisia's eyes.

"It only takes one," she said quietly. Her gaze did not break from his.

For a suicide attack, Aurore thought. *Take out Thurinia and her fleet would scatter. And yet two ships wouldn't do it, not if Thurinia had five or six. She'd take out Antisia before she got close. Unless there was a distraction...*

"Void take me," Aurore whispered. She had it. In that moment she knew exactly what to do. "What if you didn't have to put crews on the other four ships?" she asked aloud. "What if they didn't have to be spaceworthy, just appear spaceworthy?"

Everyone stared at her.

"What's the good of that?" one of the fitters asked.

"We can jam sensors, right? If Thurinia sees six ships moving and seeming battle ready, she wouldn't know if only two of them were crewed. She wouldn't know the rest were shells." Aurore leaned forward. "*Cornelia* is for real. *Determination* is for real. But the others aren't. It would give Antisia the opening she needs."

Antisia nodded slowly. "It could."

"It would," Aurore said. "The others are a distraction."

Tenn looked baffled. "It might be possible to make the others look all right, but they're not going to maneuver without crews. I told you, we can't put people on them."

Bel was grinning. He'd gotten it. He knew exactly what Aurore was thinking. "Would you care to explain, Captain Melian?"

"The Altissimus Nereus Iulus, Belimar Calado, is going to fly them remotely using a Morriganian Greater Gift," Aurore said.

"Excuse me?" Tenn said.

"How is Nereus Iulus going to get a Morriganian Greater Gift?" Antisia asked.

"I have one," Bel said. "The Solaste Crown."

"Bel, no," Sura breathed.

He was going to give away the mystery, right here, right now. "The Solaste Crown controls four atmospheric drones," he said. "We interface their systems into the four unworthy ships. I fly them remotely just as I would the drones using the Solaste Crown. Not a single human needs to be aboard the ships." He looked at the fitters. "If you didn't have to make the ships safe for crews, could you get propulsion and guidance working?"

One of them threw up his hands. "I suppose! If you're abandoning the idea of basic safety! If you don't care if it explodes if it's pressurized."

"Or don't pressurize it," Aurore said. "The one in orbit you've got moored to a stationary buoy—it may have compartments that aren't sealed and if you don't need to seal them, just make them look cosmetically whole—can you do it?"

"I can do that," Tenn said. "Slap a plate on it and paint over the pitting. It wouldn't hold in jump or atmosphere and you couldn't pressurize it without danger of a breach, but it would look ok on a scan from a distance."

"That's all we need," Aurore said. "It just needs to look good."

Sura looked aghast. "Bel, you can't. You can't take apart the Phoenix of the Sun. It's a sacred relic."

Bel tilted his head. "The Warlord Khreesos left it to Lutece Calado to protect Lono. That's what I'm using it for. This is exactly the purpose for which it was intended."

"And are you the person?" she asked. Her eyes didn't leave his.

"I'm the person who can do this now," Bel said. "That's all that matters right this minute."

A smile played around her lips. "A con man."

"The biggest con of all," Bel said. "It will be a beautiful deception." He glanced at Aurore. "Can you work with the fitters, Captain Melian?"

"It would be my pleasure to assist," Aurore said.

"Altissima, does this plan meet with your approval?" Bel asked formally. "You are, after all, the commander of Calpurnia's fleet at Lono."

Her face was pale and very still. "It does."

Dian took an audible breath. Aurore glanced at her, but she said nothing.

"Then, my friends, we have a plan," Bel said. "And with the Warlord's blessing, we may yet prevail."

EVENING CAME SOFTLY. The flames in the firebowl at the Shrine gave little light as the twilight faded. Sura scattered another spoonful of incense over the coals. Another night like this, eight years ago.

She had known his step, even now after all these years. She had known who it was before he spoke. "Amari."

He had stood just outside the door, still tall and lean, though his close-cropped hair was more gray than black. "Sanius," she said, and neither of them moved. "You should not have come."

"Why?" His voice was quiet.

"It's too dangerous."

"To you or to me?" He put his head to the side, that inquisitive expression she'd always loved.

"To me. To you. Both." Somehow she'd taken a step toward him.

"You didn't come to me, so I had to come to you."

"And how do you think it looks for the Viceroy of Lono to pay a visit to the Shrine?" He wore black, but just a somber suit, nothing that showed any rank. He could have worn a naval uniform. He was entitled to it.

He gave her a mirthless smile. "This is not an official visit. And am I nothing but the Viceroy of Lono?"

"You are my husband," Sura said. "And I have taken no other."

"Nor have I married again." He came around the firebowl and sat down on the edge of the stone wall, his long legs out before him. "When people ask why I don't marry, I say that I am wedded to my career, not that I made those vows long ago to a woman I loved and have not broken them."

"We were foolish," she said.

"Maybe. The only foolish thing I've ever done in my life. Amari…"

"I am Sura, not Amari." She did not sit. At least she needed her height. "I never thought you'd return here."

"I did."

"Viceroy of Lono?"

He shrugged. "Why not? Maybe I dreamed that I'd come back one day with an office where no one could gainsay me if I said that you were my wife."

"And what will that do on Calpurnia?"

"At a certain point they must chew it and swallow," he said.

Sura could not help but smile. That sounded like him, like the old him, a twist of humor beneath formality. "You know they would not."

"I can make them." His voice was perfectly even and her smile vanished.

"You cannot. And I cannot. We were romantic children then. These are our real lives."

For a moment he looked away, into the firebowl, the blue hints at the heart of the flames. "Where is our son?"

"I don't know," Sura said. His head came up, gaze sharp. "Truthfully, I do not know. He was attending Western Archipelago University on Calpurnia. And then he dropped out and disappeared. I have no idea where he is now."

He frowned. "Western Archipelago? Who paid for it?"

"He had a scholarship. A full grant. He won it himself. He was there three years and then…" She spread her hands. "He left. He simply left. I have no idea why. I have no idea where he went."

"I was there," he said. "I lectured there last year. If I had known…"

"If you had known, then what? He has no idea who he is."

He let out a deep breath, his eyes never leaving her face. "And whose decision was that?"

"Mine," Sura said. "It was too dangerous. If anyone here had known, if the former Viceroy had known he was my son, or if the Resistance had known

he was yours…" She folded her hands in her sleeves so she would not reach for him. *"It's better for Bel to simply be an ordinary person."*

"He's a grown man. He's twenty-two, not an infant."

"I can't tell you," Sura said, *"because I don't know. You must be satisfied with that."*

And they had left it thus. Sura looked out toward the estuary shrouded in mist. She had not known. She had never guessed he was here in Tranquility. She should have.

Sura put the incense dipper down and looked toward the Effigy. "Dark Lord, why did you deceive me?"

There was no answer.

THE NEXT HOURS were a blur to Bel. At some point he took a nap in a lavishly appointed room in the Viceregal Palace to wake in evening wondering momentarily where he was. The ceiling was high and painted with strange creatures. His childhood supplied him with names: Ema and Oma, the sea serpents who guarded the Island of Beautiful Winter, one blue and one gray, their long bodies twining around unfortunate ships.

Bel got up, finding his clothes neatly steamed and hanging on a rose-gold rack at the end of the bed. There was another meal, this time with a dozen Calpurnian officers, most of Antisia's remaining staff. He did his best to be grave and solemn, the model of virtue and no less than they would expect from Iulus' son. He asked questions and listened to the answers, though the next day he could not have said what they were. It all passed in a tired haze. If he'd done it badly, someone would have said. Certainly Antisia said little, though she drank steadily and deeply. Well, he'd be drinking heavily too if he was about to make a suicide attack.

He slept that night in the same room, waking in early morning to a discreet buzz at the door. Bel floundered around until he found the communications buttons on the table. "Yes?"

"It's Aurore," she said. "Are you up? We have a meeting with the fitters in an hour."

Bel winced. "I'm up," he said. "Be out in a few minutes." He paused. It wasn't her job, but maybe she could find someone whose job it was. "Is there any chance of coffee?"

Aurore sounded amused. "I've got some. I'll have them bring another pot."

Ten minutes later Bel emerged showered and wearing clean clothes. Aurore was in the sitting room, a pressure pot and condiment set on the marble table in front of her, a cup in her hand. "You are a lifesaver," Bel said, reaching for the second cup and sitting down on the curved bench. "Who are we meeting?"

"Tenn Mari's set up a meeting with the other Innocent fitters. They've got some concerns." Aurore shrugged. "You asked me to liase with the fitters and they want to talk to you."

"Right. Sounds good." Bel took a long drink of his coffee. "Sorry, trying to get in gear here."

"No problem." Aurore sounded amused. "You've only been a prince for a day."

"Ouch." He shook his head. "Let's hope it doesn't last."

Her eyebrows rose. "Planning to resign already?"

"The Viceroy is an appointed job," he said. "It shouldn't be for life. Ultimately, there needs to be a democratically elected leader. Not this week, but soon. I told you, I don't believe in monarchies."

"You don't have to convince me," Aurore said. "We elect our guardians. It's the Lonoi resistance you have to convince."

"And everybody waiting for the Blameless Prince," Bel said, "who want me to kick all the Calpurnians off Lono."

Aurore took a sip of her coffee. "So why don't you? Surely they could just go back to Calpurnia."

Bel poured a generous dollop of almond milk in his coffee and took a drink. That was the kind of thing people said when they had no idea. "Have you ever been to Calpurnia?"

"Twice," Aurore said. "But no more than a starport pale. I didn't have a visa to leave the port."

Of course. "I went to the university there," he said. "Somebody like you couldn't exist on Calpurnia."

Aurore frowned. "I've seen plenty of female Calpurnian spacers. Altissima Antisia is a woman."

"You've seen female Calpurnian pilots and officers, but not women." Bel took another sip. The coffee was mellow and perfect. "Men are soldiers, therefore soldiers are men. Women are medics, therefore medics are women. Men are pilots, therefore pilots are men. All high-status jobs are for men and all low-status jobs are for women. Anyone who's good enough can be a man."

Aurore looked confused. "I'm not a man. I'm a woman who's a starship captain." She gestured down at her cargo pants. "I'm xalepia, but I'm certainly not a man. If I wanted to be, or if I wanted to be disson, I could do that."

"On Menaechmi," Bel said. "Not on Calpurnia. Or in the Adelphi Rim. Men have positions of responsibility and power, have short hair, wear tailored dark clothing, do not bear children or take care of them, are intellectual and disciplined, and are focused on finance, science and war. Women are caregivers and support, have long hair, wear flowing colorful clothing, bear and take care of children and elderly people, are emotional and reactive, and are focused on social contacts. All patricians are men and all plebians are women." He shrugged. "It's not just that a particular Altissima is xalepia. Personal preference has nothing to do with it. If you're genetically female and want any kind of respect, you're socially male."

"That's bizarre," Aurore said.

He shrugged again. "That's the Politist position, and they've run Calpurnia for most of the last ninety years. It's complete equality between the biological sexes. Anyone who's good enough can be a man. Anyone who isn't good enough is a woman." He took another drink. "A lot of people don't like it. That's why they leave. They're not powerful or rich, and the best they can do is go somewhere else. I don't think they should die for that."

"And the Lonoi Resistance will kill them if there's a Rising." She frowned. "But Thurinia's Social Logic."

"Social Logic is a philosophical alternative," Bel said. "We should all return to a more 'natural' state with nuclear families and definitions of function defined by genetics. It's logical. And just as restrictive but in a different direction." He leaned forward. "And then there are the Federationists, like Iulus and Antisia, who want the old cultural aristocracy with patrician families and men dominating the public sphere. I don't like any of the alternatives. But that's what we've got."

"And that's why there are so many Calpurnians living here," Aurore said thoughtfully.

"What else can you do? Create a new social philosophy, widely disseminate it through the culture until you have a plurality of belief in your philosophy, turn that into a broad social movement and have a revolution? That's a pretty tall order. I sure can't do it." Bel took a deep breath. And that was the thing that scared him, of course. "Now a lot of people will expect it. I'm going to fix it because I'm the chosen one. It's impossible."

"I don't think you have to do that," Aurore said. "Let's just take this one problem at a time. The Calado Prince can prevent the Rising and those people won't be killed or driven away. That's the first thing." She reached for his hand and squeezed it gently. "You can do that. Be Belimar Calado and do that."

"But first I've got to be Nereus Iulus for the fitters."

"True enough," she said. "This whole plan falls apart if we can't make the ships look good. Want me to come with you?"

"I'd appreciate that a lot," Bel said.

CHAPTER
TEN

THE ELECTRIC SIX-WHEELER purred through the streets of Tranquility slowly, its tinted windows allowing Bel to see out but no one to see in. Shops were just opening for the day, a man opening the metal shutters that covered the entrance at night, a display of expensive electronics behind him, the latest from Calpurnia. An orange and white cat sat in front of the next shop calmly washing one paw while two women turned the theft detectors on. A boy who surely ought to be in school at his age was filling the bottles of people in work clothes at the next front, pouring steaming tea into vacuum carafes. The flashing signs of the night had been turned off, the streets wet from the dawn rain. A group of children dashed along, identical waist pouches with the name of a school bright yellow against their blue uniforms.

There was no rain in the Adelphi Rim. He'd gone to school through a series of corridors, then caught a green line tram that ran around the perimeter of Echo Station, the inside of the tram blaring ten or twelve advertisements while he listened to his homework on his earbuds hoping it would sink in before he got there if he turned up the binaural to his subconscious. It never worked, of course. Everybody thought you could learn that way, but it poured straight in and out again no matter how expensive the prep program your parents bought. Echo Station was a world in itself, one of the eight large orbital installations that made up the belt of light around the gas giant Adel-

pha. 3.7 million people lived on Echo Station. It massed as much as a small moon, and it wasn't the largest. That was Maurya, where you could still see the sigils of the Artifix on the walls of the inner spheres. There were parks and playgrounds, allées of linden trees, even a little lake tucked into the broad, turning belts of the station. For Bel, the horizon was up. Distance sloped away, looping upward and out of sight, the lights of buildings shining through artificial night.

His father had gotten him ready for school each morning, listening while he talked and talked and talked, eggs and fried tofu in bean sauce, a sweet nut treat to put in his bag to take with him. His mother was already gone, out the door to the health data center before Bel had to leave. But his father was retired from the Calpurnian Navy. His time was his own. He took contract jobs in cargo logistics, but he could finesse his schedule so that if he was working in the afternoon, it would be on days when Bel's mother would be home before school ended.

Bel had never wondered why he didn't have brothers and sisters. Many kids didn't. Radiation was a problem, and his father hadn't just lived on the station but been in the Navy for decades. Infertility and genetic anomalies were common. Lucky, people said, to have one healthy son. Bel had been seventeen when he died of cancer. He'd held his hand while he drifted, saying goodbye as his ventilator turned off quietly, put his arms around his mother while she bent her head against his shoulder.

And less than a year later he'd left for university, a new life, a new adventure, not thinking twice about his mother left behind.

Bel took a deep breath. His real mother. Nysia was his real mother. Pally was his real father. They were the ones who had loved him as he was, not as some kind of symbol of a future they wanted. He looked out the window and swallowed. He needed to talk to his mother, to Nysia. She was Lonoi for all she'd lived in the Adelphi Rim for twenty-five years. She'd understand all this. But that was impossible. He'd gotten himself into this mess. He'd have to get himself out.

THE MEETING WASN'T at the Viceregal Palace, but hosted by the largest of the fitters, Unified Starship Workers, at Tranquility Yards. It made sense for him to come to them, both in terms of appearance and practicality. After all, they had a lot of work to do very quickly. Their conversation rooms were as unlike the palace as possible, everything sleek and black, with personal screens at each place and a 3D projector in the middle of the black glass table. Everything was as high tech as possible and geared to a Calpurnian aesthetic. The Innocent knew how to make a point, Bel thought. They were telling their best customers that they were nothing like the Lonoi.

And maybe they were making that point to him. Certainly Tenn Mari got right to it. "We've got some concerns," he said, "that go way beyond repairing the warships." He looked at one of his colleagues, an older woman with her hair cut short to show the god-mark at her temple, a star surrounded by an oval. "Leotte, would you like to speak?"

She nodded, keen gray eyes meeing Bel's. "We'd like your assurance that you intend to rule as Nereus Iulus, not Belimar Calado."

Bel took a deep breath. This whole thing would fall apart without the fitters. "Tell me more."

"We want your commitment that the laws of Lono do not apply to us. The Innocent are not subject to Lonoi civil or criminal law but only to Calpurnian law." She leaned forward. "Lonoi law is based on their original Compact designed at Landing by the travelers who settled here. It created 'an Eco-Polity striving for traditional values and ways of living, a recreation of the ancestral societies of our homeworld by their descendants, in harmony with nature and enshrining natural homeways.' We reject these values and do not recognize Lonoi homeways as compatible with our culture."

"And yet you chose to live here," Bel observed.

"We didn't," Tenn said. "Our ancestors did a hundred and fifty years ago when they fled oppression. We were invited as refugees from debt-servitude. Calpurnia has never enforced Lonoi laws on us. This was never our choice."

"Just as it was not the choice of the creators of the Compact to leave their homeworld, but that of their parents and grandparents and great-grandparents," Bel observed. "They created a society based on the traditional societies of their ancestors whose heritage they felt they had been robbed of." He shrugged. "Of course none of them had ever lived in a traditional society. They'd been three generations on the journey. It was all based on stories and vids."

"True," Leotte said. "But this is now. If the Lonoi resistance were to truly gain control of the government, we would all be criminals. Our family structures wouldn't be recognized, many people's personal relationships would be illegal, and an entire class of people who are neither male nor female would cease to exist. We don't want traditional law—natural law, homeways, ancestral wisdom—whatever you want to call it. We want Calpurnian law that assures our rights."

"If you get Altissima Thurinia and the Social Logic faction you won't like it any better," Bel said.

"We know," Tenn said. "That's why we're backing you. You're a Federationist, or at least Altissima Antisia is. But we want your assurances that you won't cut a deal with the resistance leaders that hangs us out to dry."

Bel hoped his gambler's face showed nothing. The Resistance wanted Belimar Calado. That was how he'd called off the Rising. They expected to come out on top. If they didn't…

"It's our lives on the line," Leotte said. "Our families. Our way of life. They can live however they want. But we want immunity from Lonoi law."

And we're prepared to deal with whoever will promise that. Bel knew the unspoken part. If he didn't offer it, which Calpurnian faction would? The Politists might. Certainly the Federationists would, and there were probably some who weren't as fatalistic as Antisia. He could promise it. He had no desire to cut off the Innocent. And yet he had no illusions that many of the Resistance leaders would. Many Lonoi would. They resented the Innocent at the same time that they were happy to use the spiritually polluting technology the Innocent created. Very few people, in Bel's opinion, actually wanted to live in a pre-industrial society. They just wanted someone else to maintain solar panels and power stations, and those who benefitted most were the lowest caste Lonoi who would otherwise have to do the polluting jobs. And yet they hated the Calpurnians and distaste for the Innocent ran deep. Not to mention the half-bloods like him, the thousands of people partly of one world and partly of another. They'd have no place at all.

He could promise. But if he did, he wouldn't be going anywhere any time soon. The only way Bel could enforce any deal he made would be to stay and do it. He'd have to be Belimar Calado and Nereus Iulus for a long time—years, decades, maybe all his life. He'd never get his life back.

Aurore was looking at him, her head tilted to the side. She said nothing, but her eyes said it all, cool and summing him up. *Who are you, Bel Alan?*

That was the answer, wasn't it? He was Bel Alan, raised by his mother Nysia and his stepfather Pally Alan, a former Calpurnian plebian starship crewman in the Adelphi Rim. He was a university drop-out and failed rebel. He wasn't Sanius Iulus' pawn in a long game or Sura's Blameless Prince. He was Bel Alan.

"I give you my word," Bel said. "And I'll put it in writing. I guarantee that the Innocent will not be subject to laws based on the Compact. The Innocent were not parties to the Compact and are not covered in its provisions because they did not consent to be bound by its strictures." He looked around the room. "Is that good enough for you?"

Tenn Mari nodded slowly. "I think."

Leotte was more cautious. "And if there is some future government not based on the Compact?"

"If there is some future government which is neither based on Calpurnian law or the Compact, the Innocent will be full parties to its creation." Bel met her gaze firmly. "But surely you can't expect me to guarantee every future possible government on Lono. All I can promise is in my own lifetime, or however long I have power." He glanced down the table. "If I'm overthrown tomorrow, clearly I won't be able to enforce anything."

"Which does give us another good reason to support you," Leotte said with a twist of the lips.

Bel spread his hands. "Obviously."

"If you'll put it in writing, that's good enough for me," Tenn Mari said. "If we're going to keep Social Logic out, we've got to get these ships—I won't say fixed, but sassed up."

One by one, each of the fitters got up, shaking hands and talking as they took their leave, Bel promising to get them a document by the end of the day. At last there was no one left in the meeting room but Aurore.

"Did you mean it?" she asked.

"Unfortunately," Bel said. He walked over to the windows, looking out across the yards toward the estuary, the Shrine invisible in the smog over the water. The domed tanks of a plant were venting, a white cloud escaping that might be only steam. The elevated tram went by, its orange stripe bright. One tower showed green lights, strobing to show the approach corridor to the port. "I don't feel it," he said. "I should love Lono. But I don't."

Aurore came to stand at his shoulder. "I know what you mean," she said. "It's a thing I've always been supposed to feel. I mean, I feel the responsibility every single time I look at Beira. But not the love. My dad looks out at every square meter of city and loves it. He looks at the lights and sees the people."

"And what do you see?" Bel asked.

Aurore huffed, almost a laugh. "The stars," she said.

He looked at her sideways, cropped untidy hair and luminous dark eyes. "Maybe you belong out there."

"I know I do. But I have a responsibility." She shrugged. "Just like you."

"I think the question is what you have a responsibility to," Bel said. "When you're more than one person, you have to decide which one nobody else can be."

"Like you just did." She looked at him, searching his face like she was seeing him for the first time. "I guess you won't be needing that passage to Menaechmi."

"Not unless we lose," Bel said.

Aurore shrugged. "If this doesn't work, we'll be dead."

"There's a comforting thought." Bel shook his head. "Wait, we?"

"You really think you can do this without me?"

"Yeah, probably not." Bel grinned. "What about your ship?"

"Dian can take *Golden Wanderer* to Menaechmi and come back for me later," Aurore said. "No problem."

•　•　•

Dian, of course, had other ideas. "No fucking way!" she said, pacing around the common room of *Golden Wanderer*, her blue-tipped hair still wet from the shower. "Do you actually think I'm going to just leave you with this mess? I'm going to run home and tell Dad that you've decided to have your own personal war with Calpurnia so I just said ok and left you to it? Be real."

"There is no reason for you…" Aurore began.

"There is no reason for you to stay either," Dian said. "Except you want to." She sat down on the edge of the table. "Admit it. You want to."

Aurore took a deep breath. "You're right," she said. "I want to. All my life I've wanted to do this—to command a starship in battle. And ok, I'm not in command of a ship, but I'm here and I'm part of it. I know a whole lot more about starships and what they can do than Bel does. It's my idea and my plan. I want to see it through."

"Ok," Dian shrugged. "But you're not doing it without me."

"This is not…"

"I'm not your annoying baby sister tagging along," Dian said. "You're not getting rid of me. And if it comes to a fight, I'm the one who got packed off to the Defense Forces to dry out, remember?"

"You're no warrior, Dian."

"No, but I've had basic training, which is more than you've had," she pointed out. "You might be the best armchair admiral Menaechmi has, but have you ever actually hit someone with an energy flail?"

"No, and if I have to, this plan will have completely failed," Aurore said.

"Point." Dian pushed her hair back. "So I'm staying and *Golden Wanderer* is staying so you've got a getaway ship if you need one. And no, I'm not about to get into a battle between frigates with a merchanter with two missile tubes. That's stupid. But I'm not going to run out of here now like most of the merchant traffic, Lady bless them. I'm going to wait and see what happens so at least I can tell Dad if you get killed."

"I'm not going to get killed," Aurore said, though it was a kind of disconcerting that Dian was expecting it.

"Good, because then I'd have to be the heir of House Melian."

"And you'd hate that," Aurore said, getting up and going to the food unit. There must be something good to eat around here.

"Actually, I'd love it, but not enough to try to get you killed for it."

Aurore turned around. Dian was sitting on the edge of the table without an iota of irony in her voice. "What?"

"I said, I'm not trying to get you killed."

"The other part," Aurore said. "You'd actually want to be the heir?"

"Of course I would." Dian lifted her chin. "It's a shit show full of nutty bees, but they're my infernal nutty bees. I wouldn't be like Dad, with variable shipping rates and commodities prices on the interstellar market in my head. You've got to have the commodities before you can ship them. And they're not just numbers on a board. They're real things, not just tons of corn and oranges. Great-granddad may have built a shipping fleet, but Granddad bought farms. He invested in fishing boats and vineyards and orchards and small businesses in town. We're still eating our shares of those ventures. But they're finite, and a bunch of the contracts will be up in the next ten years. If we had to buy everything at market rates, think what that would do to the bottom line! Dad can speculate in coffee futures because we know that every morning we're getting shares from fishing boats and every harvest we're filling warehouses with shares from the farms."

"And what would you do?" Aurore asked bemusedly.

"I'd renew the contracts or look for others at favorable terms, long-range not short. The goal's not to make a wad of cash. The goal's to make sure the House eats for the next twenty to forty years no matter what else happens. We can speculate and play with the surplus, but I'd make sure we're not buying anything but luxuries at market prices." She tossed her head. "And I'd stuff it down the Best People's throats and light it on fire. I wouldn't play footsie with the old houses. I don't need their votes because I'd never be Guardian. I'd screw them over coming and going and next time there's a downturn they can buy food from us if they want to eat. At market prices."

"You really mean that." All those things, agricultural contracts and fishing shares, that were the most boring things in the world to her… "You're really interested in them."

"No shit."

"You and Dad would make a good team," Aurore said. It was a liberating thought.

"He doesn't think so," Dian said.

"He will," Aurore said. She could see the way plainly. "If I told him I wasn't going to do it, he'd have to get on board with you and he'd find out you were really good."

"And you could captain House Melian merchanters for the rest of your life," Dian said. "You could run the starships however you wanted and I could run the House and the House ventures."

It was a wonderful plan. Maybe it wasn't being Warlady, but it was a much better future than wandering around farms trying to look serious and knowledgeable while the farmer explained something about the ground and why that meant they needed money for something or other. She'd spend her life in space, never anchored to Beira with the iron chain of responsibility. "Now we just have to get Dad to see it," Aurore said. She put out her hand, little finger uppermost like a child. "Pinky shake?"

"The most sacred agreement known to humans," Dian said solemnly, just as they had as children. They shook on it.

TRANQUILITY YARDS SEETHED like a kicked anthill. The fitters were in double overtime and surely everyone in Tranquility knew it. The port was as well, though it was doubtful there were any more outbound tickets to purchase. Every passenger vessel and merchanter was fully booked and crowds of Calpurnian citizens were camping in the terminals, trying to find some way out of what was increasingly looking like a war about to happen. Antisia had needed to prompt Bel to enhance security. It was the Viceroy's job to prevent rioting, though it didn't look so good for his first act to be keeping desperate people off ships. Still, if everyone rushed the port, nobody would get off. He'd suggested halting traffic, but even if that were morally permissible, Antisia had made the case it wasn't strategically desirable. Let Thurinia know that she was preparing to resist with formidable effort! It would be ideal if many of these personally recorded vids from the terminals were shared at home. It made the Federationists look anything but beat, and nobody outbound was getting anywhere near close enough to get photos of the ships under repair which might belie the story.

Unfortunately, she was. *Cornelia* was in orbit docked with orbital tenders, but *Determination* was grounded in the yards, and it behooved Antisia to inspect the ship personally. She went aboard with five of her officers and two of the fitters. They showed her through the corridors, the smell of hot metal ever-pervasive where repairs were being conducted. It was all she could do not to shiver. Cold panic descended the moment they were through the airlock. It took every ounce of discipline she had to walk calmly through, stepping over power cables strung along the floors, speaking politely to techs who explained what they were doing. She knew she seemed stern and aloof. The alternative was hysterical.

Antisia made the tour as short as possible, trying not to gulp clean air when they ventured back out through the ventral boarding ramp.

"It's coming along," Lieutenant Tarn said. He was one of the few survivors of *Cornelia*'s command crew. She supposed he was the second most senior officer now.

"We'll be ready," the fitter said. Antisia couldn't remember his name, though she'd been introduced twice.

"So will we," Tarn said. His mouth was set in a firm line. If he had any doubts about a suicide attack, he hadn't voiced them. He'd been married, Antisia remembered. His wife had been on another ship, one destroyed at Morrigan.

"Indeed," Antisia said. It wasn't profound but at least it was resolute. "I'd like a look at the exterior." A reasonable request, and one that didn't involve going aboard again.

They walked around beneath the ship, the fitter showing them where an exterior panel had been replaced. *Determination* did need to be spaceworthy, since it was one of two ships that could be made so. They were standing beneath the ventral missile tube when someone called the fitter on his headset and he stepped away to take the call.

Tarn reached up, touching the cold metal skin with what was almost a caress. "Will Nereus Iulus be aboard?"

"*Determination*? I should think," Antisia said. "He'll need to control the other ships and I don't know what the range is." Surely not millions of kilometers.

"I'd like to meet him," Tarn said, still looking up. "I think all of *Cornelia*'s crew would."

Her last crew. The crew that prepared to die. "Yes," Antisia said, pleased her voice was steady. "I'll make certain of that."

"Is he much like the Autarch?" Tarn asked.

"Yes," Antisia said. "And no. He looks quite a bit like him—same height, same eyes—and his voice is similar. It's clear he's intelligent and takes his responsibilities seriously."

"But?"

Antisia sighed. "He lacks gravitas."

"That might not be a bad thing," Tarn said. He was still looking up at the hull. No one else was close enough to hear. "Do you believe that when we die the Lady of the Void takes us in her care? That she remembers those lost in space?"

What kind of question was that? No good Calpurnian asked that, not since her temples had been closed after the Just War. A Federationist might clandestinely worship the Lord of the Dance, but the Lady of the Void was a step too far. And yet, in that moment in *Cornelia*'s command center, in the heat of the battle, in full hull breach as she held her breath, Antisia's thought had been 'Void take me,' the old commendation of her soul. She and Tarn and Sedeli had been the only survivors of the command crew.

"Yes," she said. "I do." She put her hand on Tarn's shoulder. "So let us try to be worthy of her grace."

BEL PINCHED the bridge of his nose and looked across the expanse of Altissimus Iulus' desk to the case holding the Solaste Crown. It glittered on its black velvet pedestal. "Who am I seeing next?" he asked the hovering aide. Aurore was getting the control pods from the drones installed in the other ships, an exercise he'd left to her and the fitters since he knew absolutely nothing about retrofitting starships. Hopefully they were nearly done. They had been more than twenty hours skipping around between the yards and the orbital moorings.

Meanwhile, he was well into the next morning and it seemed everybody in Tranquility needed to meet with him.

"The Elder of Tranquility, the Elder of Reconciliation Island and the Elder of Green Crossing," the aide said. Three mayors, and all of major centers.

"I'll be delighted to see them," Bel said. "Will you have a traditional Lonoi tea service sent up?" Time to be Belimar Calado rather than Nereus Iulus. He stood up to greet them.

The first was stout and middle aged, though his dark eyes were sharply assessing. "Tonio Janelin, Elder of Tranquility," he said, taking Bel's hand in the Calpurnian manner. "And this is Law Merete from Reconciliation Island and Diyah Carpenter of Green Crossing." The other two were younger, Merete in Calpurnian clothes and Carpenter in green and gold traditional trousers and wrapped top.

"I hope that you'll join me for tea," Bel said politely. "We must all come to know one another, as I have spent much time in Tranquility, but never moved in such exalted circles."

"Though I understand you've spent some in revolutionary ones," Carpenter said. She lifted her chin. "Do you represent the Resistance?"

"Or rather, does the Resistance represent you?" Janelin asked. Moderate, pragmatic, Janelin had never been a friend to the Resistance. No doubt he'd thought the Blameless Prince was a myth. Well, so had Bel.

"No one represents me," Bel said candidly. "And as for who I represent, I believe that my job is to do the best I can for everyone on Lono, regardless of their party or beliefs."

He thought he saw Merete's shoulders relax a little.

"Including the Innocent and the half-Lonoi?" Carpenter asked.

This was not the time for lying. "Yes," Bel said. "And the Calpurnians who live here. I am half-Lonoi, son of Amari Calado and Sanius Iulus. I didn't ask for this, but having inherited the responsibility, I will serve everyone to the best of my ability." He took a breath. "I wasn't raised in a palace. I wasn't raised as an Altissimus. All I can bring to this is my own life. And my determination not to fail."

Janelin and Carpenter shared a look. "There are many," Carpenter said carefully, "especially in the outlying isles like Green Crossing,

who think that Lonoi who consort sexually with Calpurnians are trai-
tors. They should be shaved and sent to a retreat for a decade of repen-
tance. They're collaborators. Any child so conceived should be
aborted."

"Obviously I don't support aborting myself," Bel said. It had not
quite occurred to him what Sura had faced.

"She mentions it to clarify why there are many Lonoi who won't
support you," Janelin said. "They're not with the Resistance and they
have very little contact with Calpurnians or the Innocent. They'll see
you as a misbirth, the product of an illicit liaison which should have
never been allowed to come to term."

"I'm afraid that's their problem," Bel said, keeping his voice bland
and light.

"If you truly intend to govern Lono for everyone who lives here,
that includes them," Merete said. "You must benefit them and care for
them as paternally as everyone else. And we are not talking about
some tiny minority. If we were to once again have a Council of Elders
such as advised the Calado Princes before the Calpurnian takeover,
they would clearly make up as much as a third of a democratically
elected Council."

"Less than that if the Innocent and the Calpurnian expatriates also
elect Council seats," Bel said. "I intend to see those populations fairly
represented as well."

Janelin blinked. "They have never…"

"No," Bel said. "They haven't had representation before. When I
said everybody who lives here, I mean everybody. Which means Tranquility and other centers will elect Innocent or people of mixed blood
or Calpurnian expatriates."

Carpenter put her head to the side. "You really think you can shove
that down people's throats? The whole goal of the Resistance has been
to reclaim Lono for Lonoi. To return to the pure terms of the Compact."

Bel's hands tightened under the table, though his voice was still
light. "The Compact was created two thousand years ago by voyagers
who wished their grandparents had never left our homeworld. They'd
never lived in a traditional society. They were born on the generation
ships. They created an idealized version of a traditional society based

on stories and media. The idea that we are bound by their dreams for all eternity is idiotic. We are here and now, not in some make-believe utopia disgruntled star voyagers imagined."

Janelin cleared his throat. "Most Lonoi—a very large majority—on the other islands want to return to the Compact. If you want a democratic government, you can't make 70 or 80 percent of them agree to something else except the way the Calpurnians have, which is by force."

"I can tell you for certain that none of the rest of us are for that," Merete said. "We will not turn on our fellow Lonoi."

"I'm certainly not suggesting any kind of military action," Bel said. "I'm just saying that a representative Council must represent everybody. I know the Innocent have never had representation, but that's how it is." *Politics, he thought, was a lot like a high stakes card game. Time to see what they had in their hands.* "So, unless I govern as Sanius Iulus rather than Belimar Calado, they're going to have to get on board."

And trade one Calpurnian Viceroy for another. Which would put them back at square one.

"Of course we'd prefer Belimar Calado," Merete said. "We're simply pointing out some of the challenges that you face."

"I'm aware of that," Bel said with a friendly smile. *Nothing in those hands but low numbered cards. That's what he'd thought.* "So right now we need to pull together against Altissima Thurinia, who will attempt to reestablish Calpurnian sovereignty. If we don't succeed in doing that, these other discussions become academic."

"Understood," Janelin said. "It's been informative."

CHAPTER
ELEVEN

BEL ALAN CAME aboard *Cornelia* in his best black suit, the double-breasted raw silk suit he'd worn to the reception to meet Altissima Antisia for the first time, severe and Calpurnian. He had carefully checked his appearance in the mirror, made certain of the sharpness of his mustache and haircut. Nereus Iulus was a young man of good family, a young man who was going places. He did not wear a uniform. To pretend he was Navy would be ridiculous. He was an altissimus, and properly respectful of everyone in their sphere.

Cornelia was moored to an orbital dock, tech crews in spacesuits swarming over her surface, testing every square centimeter for hull integrity. *Cornelia* had taken one massive missile hit aft, and while that breach and the surrounding compartments had been repaired over the last few months, the deformation stress was bound to have damaged seals on panels nowhere near the site. Still, there was a fully pressurized route to the command center and all the comm equipment was working properly. An aide followed after him, a dark padded case holding the Solaste Crown, Sura bringing up the rear.

A Calpurnian officer about his own age met him at the airlock. "Officer of the Watch Tarn, Altissimus," he said. "It's an honor. The Altissima's shuttle has not yet arrived."

"An honor on my part as well," Bel said gravely. "I'd like to see your command center. I'm sure Altissima Antisia will be here soon." He walked at his side through the corridors. Here and there patches were readily apparent. No need to make it look nice on a ship that was about to make a suicide attack. Bel tried not to shiver. The man next to him would be dead soon. He made himself pay suitable attention to Tarn's words.

"...and down here is the ship's mess. Not that we'll need it for more than a last meal or two. They say even prisoners get that," Tarn said with black humor.

Bel stopped, the entourage stopping too, trying not to crowd. "Why are you doing this?" he asked in a low voice.

Tarn's gray eyes met his frankly. "Why not? I've got nothing to live for."

"Why this?" Bel said gently. Sura couldn't hear. He drew Tarn a little further away.

The corner of Tarn's mouth twitched. "Because others do. There are people with families on Lono. Wives. Husbands. Kids. Even parents. Thurinia will send everybody to reeducation camps at best. If we can take her out, maybe you can make some kind of deal with whoever comes next."

"You think?"

"I think somebody has to." Tarn shrugged. "Maybe it's you. Maybe it's not. But we've been tearing ourselves apart for a hundred and fifty years. One faction, then another. Federationists, Politists, and now Social Logic. I don't know why we're broken. I just know we've got to stop Thurinia because Social Logic isn't the answer."

Bel nodded slowly. "I came to that conclusion myself at the university." Tarn was like so many he'd known there. "I'm not a Federationist. I'm not a Politist. There's got to be some other answer."

"Maybe you can find it. I don't know. But somebody's got to try. Somebody's got to fix us. Heal us. You've got as much chance as anybody."

"So do you," Bel said.

"We'll do the job," Tarn said. "The Altissima won't back down. We'll get it done."

"Of course," Bel said. *No emotion. It wasn't in character.* He took a deep breath. "Show me the command center."

TARN HAD SHOWED him most of the stations before Altissima Antisia arrived. She looked pale and shaky, coming into the command center with Aurore and Dian Melian behind her.

"We're done with the drone installation," Aurore said. "The Altissima was kind enough to pick us up from *Gallant*. It's ready. Anytime you want to cast it off from the buoys, you can test the guidance."

"No one is still aboard?" Bel asked.

"No, we brought the installation crew with us," Aurore said. "Like I said, we're done. *Determination* is almost ready to launch with a crew, and the other four are now drone operated." She held up her crossed fingers. "I think everything's working. You'll need to get them launched, and that's on you and the crown."

"Good. Thank you." Bel looked over at the aide carrying the smooth black case that held the Solaste Crown. Now that it came to it, he felt an odd reluctance to open it, to touch it again. *Don't be silly,* Bel thought. *It can't make you into Belimar Calado. It's just a thing. It doesn't have a mind of its own.* The aide held the case and Aurore began to unfasten it, latches on two sides that then folded down, showing the crown on its velvet stand. A sigh ran around the command center. Its long strands of gold swayed gently. Bel swallowed. He'd come this far. He had to put it on. Everyone was waiting. *The Autarch put it on,* he thought. *Surely he tried it on. It didn't make him do anything. He was the Autarch's son. If it was all about genetic links, that was as true as that he was the Calado heir.* Bel lifted it carefully from the stand and put it on his head.

There was a moment of disorientation, as though he'd moved too fast and his balance was trying to catch up, but this time there was no vision of the drones, no vision of Tranquility or the crowds. And how should there be? The crown was no longer connected to the drones beneath the Shrine. The drones' systems were now implanted in each of the hulk ships, supposedly integrated with their controls. Bel let out a breath he hadn't been aware of holding. He needed to isolate one. He needed to find one of the ships clearly, to try to touch its sensors the way he'd used the drone's sensors. One strand. One ship. How was this supposed to work anyway? One ship.

It was as though he looked down on Lono from above, a chain of green islands set amid dark blue seas, lambent azure shapes showing shallow water. Light reflected off the water at the horizon. The shadows of a few clouds skimmed across the waves. Water. Light. Green and growing things. It was like music deep inside, swelling heartbeat of water against shore, of air against void. Beyond the rim of the world, stars rose in the indigo sky, constellations to aid sailors, destinations and dreams beyond imagining, a sea far broader than the whispering one beneath. Like an exhalation. Like a breath from deep in his chest made into a note, it sang out of him. It sang of winds and water, trees and rocks beneath the sky, the towers of Tranquility rising into the night, the soft sound of snowflakes falling on cherry trees, the crackle of flames. There, before the Shrine, beneath the trees, petals turned to smoke in the fire-bowl. He stood there rapt, caught in yearning for the skies which could not answer...

"They took her from me."

Bel turned around. A man his own age stood beside the fire, with a scarred face and a harp beneath his arm. "They locked her out there and closed the doors. They tried to stop every chink she might slip through, every symbol, every whisper. They tore open their chests and cut out their hearts and then wondered why they could not love." He came around and sat down on the stone wall, looking out over estuary and mist-shrouded sea. "What is left to me but vengeance?"

"I don't understand," Bel said.

He put his harp in his lap. "Your father came here. He came here to ask for the initiation he could not find on Calpurnia. He made the Accusation against himself and asked for grace, but I have none to give. The hounds are loosed, and I may not call them back."

"You are the Lord of the Dance," Bel said.

"So they called me. I do not dance now. This harp is silent." He tilted his head back, light eyes reflecting the distant stars. "She cannot hear me."

"My father received initiation?" Bel asked. "A Calpurnian Altissimus?" Forbidden didn't even begin to cover it…

"For all the good it did him." He shrugged. "The hounds will run until the world is fire beneath their feet. Until Calpurnia suffers the same fate as Inanna. Your father thought he could turn that fate, but it is not possible. The blood of the five hundred million dead of Inanna is on your hands, and on your hands it will remain until Calpurnia has paid the debt ten times over. Blood for blood. Life for life."

Bel shivered. "What can stop it?"

"Your father asked the same thing. I give you the same answer: nothing." He smiled like a wolf. "So take your fleet and kill Thurinia. Bring them down in fire. The frozen blood of your brothers will fall on Lono like rain. Do what you were born to do. Kill."

Everything went black, like a screen resetting, then stabilized. Bel looked out through the sensors of one of the ships moored to a geostationary buoy, its control systems online though atmospherics were red.

The ship. That's what I was doing. The ship. Focus, Bel, he thought. It was waiting for instructions. *Cast off from the buoy,* Bel thought at it. *Retract the docking lines.*

Slowly, sluggishly, it responded. One line detached, then another. They reeled in meter by meter.

"Are you all right?" There was a voice from far away.

Bel opened his eyes. Aurore was watching him closely, her hand on his shoulder. They were in the command center. Not the ship. Not the Shrine. "Yeah," he said quietly. "It just takes a lot of concentration." Everyone was watching him nervously. He raised his voice. "*Gallant* has cast off from the mooring buoys. It's working. It's just kind of slow. The drones' cores weren't meant to do this. I'm taking my time and getting the hang of it."

That seemed to satisfy everyone. Aurore looked visibly relieved. "Well, of course there's a learning curve."

"I'm getting it," Bel said. "I'm going to move *Gallant* to a high geostationary orbit and practice with maneuvering thrusters before I try getting anything to take off."

"Sounds like a plan," Aurore said.

"Is there any way I can assist?" Tarn asked.

"A chair would help," Bel said. He resisted the urge to wipe sweat off his brow. This was not the time to think about the rest or how profoundly unnerving it had been.

It was several hours before Bel was able to put aside the Solaste Crown, and by then his head was throbbing. Still, he'd managed to get the damaged ships launched and into a stable orbit, with *Gallant* riding at a respectable stationkeeping distance from *Cornelia*. It didn't look like a hulk on sensors.

"You need some food," Aurore said, and hustled him into what must normally be a lounge not far from the command center. He lay down on the couch and closed his eyes. Just a moment. Just a moment of rest.

He woke as Aurore opened heated ration packets, their familiar scents making his stomach growl.

"Here," she said, thrusting a tiny packet of liquid analgesic into his hand. "Drink up. Then have some food."

"I didn't mean to go to sleep," Bel said. He winced and gulped it down.

"You were only out twenty minutes." Aurore opened a packet of rehydrated potatoes with cheese sauce. "Pretty intense, huh?"

"You can't imagine." Bel popped an identical packet open and reached for a spoon. Maybe Aurore wouldn't think it was crazy. He didn't look at her face. "I saw the Lord of the Dance."

"What?"

Now he did glance at her, her head to the side, a quizzical but not skeptical expression on her face. "This is what happened. Or what seemed to happen."

He told her the whole thing while they ate potatoes and then opened another ration packet. Aurore looked thoughtful. "You believe me?"

"My father is the Husband of the Golden Lady," Aurore said. "Of course I believe you. Talking to gods happens all the time in my family."

"Not in mine," Bel said. "Except apparently it does!" He threw up his hands, spoon in one. "I don't have any idea what to do with this."

"Well, it's a classical curse," Aurore said. "Or that's what it sounds like. The hounds are loosed and they pursue everyone who did whatever the thing is."

"Isolate Inanna," he said grimly. "But that was a hundred and fifty years ago. There's no one on Calpurnia who made that decision! There's no one who was even alive when it was made. If the curse was on the people who did that, they're all dead. They've been dead for decades. There isn't anything that anyone can do about it now."

"Send the Innocent back to Inanna?" Aurore mused.

"The Innocent don't want to go," Bel said. "And why should they? Their ancestors were offered asylum as refugees five or six generations ago. Lono is their home. Forcibly repatriating them to somewhere they've never been would just be another crime."

"That can't be the answer then," she said. "What is it that keeps making the curse happen? What else happened?"

"Calpurnians killing Calpurnians?" Bel sighed. "We've been tearing each other apart for more than a hundred years. The Internal Wars go on and on, faction against faction. External wars too."

"And every time a faction kills a bunch of people, their friends and relatives plan vengeance," Aurore said. "And then they kill the first faction's people, and around you go again. Everybody has someone they've lost. Everybody has a reason for vengeance."

"And the Lonoi do. And the Innocent do. If Iulus couldn't think of a way to stop this, I don't know how I can. Obviously getting everybody together to attack Morrigan wasn't the answer!"

"Clearly not." Aurore frowned. "It seems like the thing you need to do is avoid spilling any blood."

"How am I supposed to defeat a battlefleet without spilling any blood?" Bel demanded.

"We stopped the Rising without spilling blood," she pointed out.

"So far," Bel said, "but Thurinia is not going to be willing to negotiate. She's coming to stake a claim. And sure, we could still try to evacuate, but we know all the problems with that. And that would mean abandoning Lono to Thurinia." He took a bite of his rations. "The only way to stop Thurinia is to take her out. Antisia has a plan that might work if we can get her the opening."

"And then Antisia and her crew die, and Thurinia and her crew die, and the curse goes on." Aurore frowned. "Blood spilled in the void. It's not supposed to be like that. The Lord of the Dance is the lord of life. He's a generative principle. Rain and vegetation and good soil."

"Not anymore," Bel said. "And remember, nobody on Calpurnia is supposed to take him seriously."

"Maybe that's part of the problem."

Bel sighed. "Maybe, but I don't see what I can do about that either. How am I supposed to do this without bloodshed?"

She frowned. "A bluff, obviously."

"We're already bluffing that we have a fleet when we don't."

"What if we do exactly what we were going to do, only not make the suicide run?" Aurore asked slowly. "We've got the drone control working. It will look like we have six ships. What if you push Thurinia to stand down? She can jump out with no harm done. Would she rather fight to the death at even odds or fold? You're the gambler. Lono's not her world. Folding doesn't lose her anything. Can't you get an opponent to fold if it's the safe move?"

"Maybe," Bel said. There was a spark there, an idea. "If it looks good enough and I can play it right."

"Then we try it," Aurore said. "What's to lose?"

"If it doesn't work and she sees through the bluff, Antisia's lost her chance. The only way she can take out Thurinia is to go straight for her while she's distracted by the hulks."

"That could still happen," she said. "If she sees through it, we're finished. It's just a bigger gamble."

"But if we win, we do it without anybody dying." Not Tarn. Not any of this crew. "Double or nothing," Bel said.

BEL WENT BACK out into the command center with Aurore, who joined her sister at one of the side plots where she seemed to be looking at the orbital docking facilities. Altissima Antisia was sitting quietly in the command chair, her eyes on the armscreen swung across her body. "Altissima, if I might have a word with you?"

"Of course, Viceroy." She got to her feet and followed him back into the lounge, not a hair out of place, her voice utterly cool. Bel had never been able to manage that kind of gravitas. The door closed behind them.

"I've been thinking," Bel said. "I believe we can effectively warn off Thurinia without the necessity of a suicide attack."

Antisia's eyebrows rose. "How can we possibly do that?"

"If we appear to have six functional ships, and she has no more than seven and possibly fewer, I think I can get her to pull back. After all, if she fights on even odds even if she wins, she will take heavy losses. Perhaps she'll be killed herself. Almost certainly she'll lose the greater part of her strength. It should be possible, in her surprise at seeing your fleet battleready, and my claim as Viceroy of Lono or the Calado Prince, to get her to reconsider and retreat until she's got a better chance of a clear victory." Bel was proud of how well he'd put it.

Antisia frowned. "But then she will pull back and consolidate. She won't be defeated or killed. We will have to deal with Thurinia and Social Logic again at a time that's more advantageous for them. The only way to win is to take her out."

"Which it's not certain we can do," Bel said. "I know you would try, but it's possible that your crew's sacrifice would be in vain. We could hardly have a worse situation for us."

"And who is us?" Antisia asked. "The Federationist faction? The world of Lono?"

"Us. You and me right here," Bel said. "We're at every disadvantage, two ships on six or seven with limited missiles. Yes, she'll live to fight another day. And so will we. We benefit more than she does from delay."

"I don't agree," Antisia said. "She will have Calpurnia and all the forward bases."

"And what is the situation on Calpurnia?" Bel said. "We don't know. But the Federationists and the Politists haven't just disappeared.

It's fluid. That's why I'm making the decision to bluff her rather than risk everything on a suicide attack that might not work."

"I understand," Antisia said. "Very well, Altissimus. Is that all?"

"Certainly," Bel said. "Now I'm going over to *Determination* with the Solaste Crown to finish getting the ships into position. I know you'll be ready to play your part when Thurinia gets here."

"I will be," Antisia said.

AURORE FOLLOWED Bel and his entourage, including the aides carrying the Solaste Crown, to the shuttle to take them over to *Determination* and then to take Dian and any nonessential techs back down to Tranquility. The corridors were still heavily masked with plastic seals here and there where compartments behind weren't tight. Maybe if they survived this confrontation, the fitters would be able to do something better. Aurore shook her head mentally. She wasn't sure she'd ever be comfortable going to jump in *Cornelia* even with an extensive refit. There had been so much structural damage.

As they turned the last corner before the airlock, Dian grabbed her wrist and pulled her back. "I need to talk to you."

"What's going on?" Aurore said.

Dian's voice was low and urgent. "Victoria's not going through with it. She's still planning a suicide attack."

"She agreed." Aurore let the rest of the party get around the corner. "What makes you think she's not on board? Did she say so?"

"She said goodbye," Dian said. "I know. You have to trust me on this."

"Why would she do that?" Their hands were tight on each other's wrists. "The plan's changed. We've got another way."

"The other way is crazy!" Dian said. "Look, you and I think it could work because it's a Dad Plan. We do this kind of shit. We trick and we bluff and we play one thing against another and twist and turn. We know it can work. Calpurnians don't do this! Victoria doesn't believe it can work. She thinks the straight out go-for-the-throat suicide attack is the only winning card! She's going to play it her way no matter what she told Belimar or whatever his name is!"

Aurore glanced back down the corridor to where Bel's group must have surely reached the airlock. "We need to stay aboard," she said.

"Damn right." Dian pursed her lips.

"I'll be back." Aurore let go and hurried to the airlock. As she'd thought, they'd all boarded the shuttle except for one aide who was nervously waiting at the airlock. "Excuse me," Aurore said, brushing past him and finding Bel with her eyes. He was sitting in the front seats in the passenger compartment, the ones with the most leg room, the seat next to him left open for her.

She leaned into the row and he looked up and smiled. "Ready to go?"

"No," she whispered, bending over him. "Antisia is going to play this her way. I need to stay and keep her on task."

For a wonder Bel didn't argue. He just nodded sharply. "Understood. Do what you need to do. I'll back you up."

"Thank you." For a moment their eyes met, their faces inches apart. Intent, serious, vulnerable—she had the sudden urge to kiss him. Which was ridiculous. That wasn't the kind of thing she did. "I've got this," Aurore said, and hurried back to the airlock, not looking to see if he turned around to watch her go. She addressed the aide at the airlock. "You can cast off," she said. "My sister and I are staying aboard." She watched the airlock cycle before she went to find Dian.

OF ALL THE CALPURNIAN SHIPS, *Determination* was in the best shape, Bel thought as they approached. It hadn't taken major damage in the battle, just minor scrapes, though it only had ten missiles left. The captain had exhausted most of his ordnance against Morrigan's fleet before exchanging fire with an orbital station and then pulling out when the general withdrawal order was given. Bel went aboard in his sharp black suit, hopefully not too creased and worse for wear by now.

They'd set aside the best cabin for him to wash and shave and eat something. It wouldn't do for the crew to see him engaged in such mundane tasks. It was quiet and dimly lit, the Solaste Crown in its case on the little desk. Bel took a deep breath. Best to wash and eat and drink while he could. Who knew when he'd get the chance again?

He'd managed a few mouthfuls when the chime rang. "Altissimus, we are detecting a gravitational anomaly in the outer system."

Which meant that a ship was preparing to come out of jump. It might be simply a merchant ship inbound to Lono. Or not. "On my way," Bel said, grabbing the crown's case and hurrying out to the command center.

By the time he reached it, the screens were split between a visual and a plot of the system. *Determination*'s captain stood up. "Altissimus, we have six ships coming out of jump. Mass and configuration suggest three ships of the line and three frigates."

"So nearly even," Bel said. In theory, they had two ships of the line and four frigates.

"As you say," the captain said wryly. After all, he knew that only two ships were operable.

"Time for me to move the other ships into position," Bel said. He opened the crown's case and put it on without stopping to think this time. There was a swirl of sensation, data from all four cores pouring in, like different colored strands leading back to a center. Bel pulled one out, thinking his command, *engines ahead at one quarter power*. And another. *Engines ahead at one quarter power with a slight turn to port.* Thurinia needed to see the ships maneuvering. He'd bring them up slightly, each a little differently. Eyes closed, Bel concentrated on the interface.

AURORE HURRIED BACK to *Cornelia*'s command center. The doors opened ahead of her, Dian a step behind. Antisia was standing by her couch, one hand on the headrest, her eyes on the screen. "Tarn, give me full engine power. Hold prepared for full speed ahead." On the double screens before them one showed *Determination*, and the other a full plot of the ships. "Remani, have you identified which one is Thurinia's flagship?"

"Not yet, Altissima," one of the officers replied.

"Tarn, as soon as we have a positive identification…"

"…you'll go to ramming speed?" Aurore interrupted. "That is not the plan."

Antisia spun around. The look of horror on her face when she saw Dian was unfeigned. "You're not supposed to be here."

"Because you're making a suicide run?" Dian said hotly. "That's not what you agreed to."

"It has to be." Antisia was pale but her voice didn't shake.

"It isn't necessary," Aurore said, acutely aware of the ship's officers around them. Some of them wore regulation energy flails at their belts. She was unarmed. She'd have to persuade them as well as Antisia. "Belimar—Nereus Iulus—is going to bluff her. She doesn't know who he is and she doesn't know what strength he has or what Lono has. She's going to be wrong-footed. All it will take is a good push to get her to withdraw."

"And then what?" Antisia demanded. "This is our one chance."

"A head-on assault? One ship against six? Do you really think you can close before this ship is destroyed?" Aurore said. "Look at the ordnance! Do you think structural integrity will hold when the ship is hit with two or three 500s? It will break apart. You won't make it through to ram. They've got countermeasures for your missiles and you will never cover that distance before *Cornelia* is destroyed."

"There is no other choice!"

"Live to fight another day at better odds!" Aurore said. "We can't win. But we can come out of this without Lono falling to Thurinia. We bluff her into withdrawing. Time is our friend, not hers!"

Antisia's eyes were bright with unshed tears. "Do you think I want to do this? This is my duty. This is our duty. It's our last duty."

"Your duty is to obey your lawful orders," Aurore snapped. She thought she had enough authority in her voice. "Communications, open a channel to *Determination*."

The man's habit of obedience was strong. Bel shifted into focus on the screen beside the plot, his brow furrowed, the Solaste Crown in his hands. "Yes?"

Aurore drew herself up. "Altissimus, Altissima Antisia refuses your direct order to follow the plan we laid out in conference." She hoped Bel understood what she was saying. Antisia couldn't back down even if she wanted to, not unless Bel made it inescapable.

Bel's mouth twitched. "Altissima, my orders were plain. There is to be no suicide attack."

"There is no other choice," Antisia began.

"Altissima, by my authority as Viceroy of Lono, you are hereby relieved of your command. Captain Melian, you are appointed Captain of the Calpurnian Naval Vessel *Cornelia*, your duty to begin immediately."

Aurore looked at the nearest member of the crew. "Escort her to the ready room and remain with her." Her eyes included Dian. A crew member might agree to whatever twists and turns Antisia might come up with. Dian wouldn't.

For a moment she thought they wouldn't do it, and then Antisia drew herself up and walked out stiffly, Dian and the crewman following.

Aurore turned back to the rest of the command crew. "Alright then. We have operational forward tubes, do we not?"

"Yes, captain," the weapons officer replied.

"Then load a pair of 500s," Aurore said. "Hold ready." She sat down on the captain's couch and pulled the control arm across her body.

BEL LOOKED at his split screens, hopefully with a resolute expression on his face. He put the Solaste Crown back in its case. He'd intended to wear it throughout, counting on having Aurore here on *Determination* with him, to handle the negotiations. Now that would not be possible. Any second now Thurinia would have taken the measure of his fleet, hopefully unable to get a solid scan, and would hail him. Should he hail her first? Or was that showing weakness? He'd wait a moment longer…

"Altissimus, we have a transmission."

"Put it on the screen," Bel said. He squared his shoulders as the screen split into thirds.

A man his own age in the scarlet uniform of the Calpurnian Navy looked at him, his dark hair precisely cut, a somewhat startled expression on his face as he saw Bel. "I am Altissimus Vipsani, Captain of the Calpurnian Naval Vessel *Makaria*. I was expecting Altissima Antisia."

"The Altissima is no longer in command," Bel said pleasantly. "I am Altissimus Nereus Iulus, son of the late Autarch, and Viceroy of Lono."

Vipsani's eyes twitched as though he were responding to something on another screen of his. *Makaria* must not be the flagship. Thurinia was on another ship and his screen was split too, Bel thought. "I was not aware that the Autarch had a son," he said cautiously.

"I intend to present my proofs, including results of genetic testing, to the Calpurnian Senate," Bel said. "In the interim, Antisia has accepted these proofs and graciously appointed me Viceroy of Lono and commander of all Calpurnian forces in the Lono system. As you see, this is a fleet of six ships."

A coup, Bel thought. *They hadn't seen one coming, they had no idea who he was, or what the situation on Lono was.* Vipsani's frown deepened. "I see."

"Unless your intentions are to place your ships under my command, as is proper given the oaths that Altissima Thurinia once made to the Autarch, you are requested to withdraw from the Lono system," Bel said.

"Altissimus, they're scanning," one of the officers said.

"Naturally," Bel said, toggling the sound off with one finger. "Hold firm. Aurore, are you on the line?"

"I am," she said from her third of the screen.

"Make whatever offensive moves you want," Bel said, "short of opening fire." He turned the sound back on as though the microphone were catching him giving orders on another screen. "*Generous* and *Viole*, hold station and do not fire without orders," he said as though speaking to two of the ships that were entirely remote. "*Cornelia*, you may respond as appropriate."

Aurore was sitting in the captain's chair. "Forward at one-quarter power," she said. "Open the forward missile tubes to vacuum but hold fire."

Vipsani's eyes moved again. His sound was off, and for a moment he ducked out of camera range. Talking to Thurinia, obviously, or getting the read on *Cornelia*. Or both.

"Another hail, Altissimus," the communications officer said.

"Put it on."

Her hair was white-blond, so closely cut it looked like feathers against the curve of her head, her eyes ice-blue. "I am Altissima Thurinia," she said.

"A pleasure," Bel said. "I have hoped to meet you, and I see no reason why there should be so much unpleasantness between us." He allowed a little smile. "Nereus Iulus."

"The Autarch Sanius Iulus had no children," Thurinia said. "You are an imposter."

"You will not say so when you have seen my proofs," Bel said. "Including the genetic tests and the certificate of marriage between my parents and the acknowledgement of my birth created and date-stamped by the Autarch himself. I forgive your skepticism. It is under-standable. I will present my proofs to the Senate in due time, just as I presented them compellingly to Altissima Antisia."

"Why is one of your ships clearing missile tubes?" Thurinia demanded.

"One of my captains is over-eager," Bel said. "All ships, hold station as ordered!" Her sound was off, and he could not spare a glance to see what Aurore was doing. Playing it, he hoped. Damn, she was a good partner!

Vipsani had turned his head, speaking to Thurinia in a way that Bel could not read his lips. Clearly they were thrown by the turn of events.

"I will ask you a second time—withdraw from the Lono system immediately. All negotiations are predicated on your immediate with-drawal." Bel hardened his voice. On the plot *Cornelia* was still inching forward on momentum though her thrusters were no longer firing.

Thurinia turned to him again. "Where is Altissima Antisia?" she asked.

Bel gave her a polite nod. "Alas, the Altissima is indisposed at the moment. Captain Melian commands *Cornelia*." Indisposed might mean dead. Or imprisoned. Or otherwise the subject of compellingly presented documents. In any event, it was clear Bel had come out on top. And who knew what he had? "I will ask you once more, and once more only, to withdraw from the Lono system."

Cornelia was opening the missile ports, a pair of 500s armed in the tubes.

Vipsani spoke. "You will give us time to plot a jump point."

"I will give you six minutes," Bel said. That was reasonable, right? Aurore would know. He cut the communication. "Aurore?"

"Armed and waiting," Aurore said.

"Is six minutes enough?"

"More than enough if they hustle," she said. "I'm loading the ventral tubes too."

Determination's captain looked at him. "Altissimus, should we load tubes as well?"

"Yes," Bel said. He was sweating down his back. "Can you turn the environmentals a little cooler?"

"In about three minutes we'll know if they're cycling engines for jump," Aurore said. "Also they'll need to come about for an exit corridor. Their current facing will put them in Lono's gravity well."

"Understood," Bel said, though he got about half of that. Three minutes. In three minutes they'd know if it was working. He made himself stand very still, his eyes on the plot. Was one of the ships turning? Were they still scanning? *Cornelia* was still in front, which would confuse their scan. They'd get her most clearly and she was the one obviously armed.

"*Makaria* is turning to port," Aurore said. "She's coming around on another heading."

"To jump or to fire?" Bel asked.

"Too soon to know."

"Clear the tubes," Bel said. "Prepare to fire."

"I have a solution on *Makaria*," Aurore said. "All missiles online."

Waiting. Waiting. Bel saw it on the screen first, a slight change in velocity.

"*Makaria*'s main engines are cycling," Aurore said. "Two others are turning onto the same heading."

"They're going to jump." Bel was nearly falling over with relief, though he didn't move.

Her eyes were still on the plot. "Looks like. Hold position. Hold firing solutions."

Vipsani's *Makaria* accelerated, followed one by one by the others, racing toward a point outside of Lono's orbit around the primary. *Makaria* winked out, disappearing into the fold of the jump, and Bel let out a breath.

When the last ship went to jump, a strange stillness enveloped everyone.

Aurore wasn't looking at him. She was looking at *Cornelia's* command crew. "Welcome back to the land of the living," she said.

THE AUTARCH'S office was exactly as Sura had expected it, austere and entirely Calpurnian. Except for the Solaste Crown. It sat in its case on the worktable, not in the glass display case which had obviously been constructed for it. Sura's red silks whispered against the carpet as she was shown in, a deferential aide closing the door behind her. Bel wore black, but his severe coat was open to show a flowered shirt in shades of indigo and pink. He looked up from his screen.

It was very strange indeed to stand in front of him like this, as though she were the suppliant. "You wanted to speak with me?"

Bel got up and came around the desk. "I did." He walked past her to the worktable and began to close the case around the Solaste Crown. "I'm delivering this into your safekeeping." He snapped the closures tight.

Sura was speechless for a moment, watching him fasten the last latch. She found her voice. "What?"

"You hired me to get the Solaste Crown." He held the case out to her. "Here it is. Our bargain is concluded."

"Bel, that was not…" Sura began.

"That was never your plan," he said evenly. "You intended for me to claim the crown all along and be the Blameless Prince." He put the case in her hands. "I'm not. I don't believe in princes or monarchies. I am not your promised one. I'm not going to restore the Calado rule or the Compact."

"What about Lonoi independence? What about everything you promised everyone?"

"I am going to preside over a temporary government to transition to multiple democratic entities," Bel said. "No more planetary rule. Before the Calado princes, Lono was a multi-state world with different groups of people living according to their preferences. It can be again. There's no reason any part of Lono needs to control how any other part lives. If separate islands choose to adopt different laws, that's their choice."

Sura heard her voice shake. "You are giving away the empire of your forebearers."

"That empire was lost long ago," Bel said. "And that's as it should be. We don't live in the time of the Warlord and the Calado Princess. That was hundreds of years ago. The various peoples of Lono are going to have to establish their own governments as they see fit."

"And just how are you going to keep Calpurnia from simply rolling over everything?" Sura demanded. "We have finally, after generations of fighting, achieved a chance at independence!"

Bel smiled a quicksilver smile. "Because I'm the Calpurnian Viceroy. I'm Nereus Iulus. I'm going to be confirmed in my father's seat in the Senate and as Viceroy will oversee the transition to Lono's democratic self-rule."

Sura put the case down heavily. "You can't. You're my son. You're the Calado Prince! You're Lonoi."

His smile faded. "Maybe if I'd been raised here, I would be. If I'd grown up with you at the Shrine. But I didn't. You sent me away."

"Bel, it was too dangerous…"

His eyes met hers, earnest and quiet rather than angry. "I grew up with parents who loved me and were proud of me, one Calpurnian and one Lonoi, Pally and Nysia Alan. I was accepted to a good university on my own merits, by my own ability and hard work, not because I was a prince. I lived on Calpurnia and I saw what it's like if you're not patrician. I lived in the Adelphi Rim. And I lived on Lono. Not as a

Calado heir, but as a half-breed nobody." He took a breath. "Now I have the chance to change things."

Sura's voice was flat. "You want to be your father's son. You never even met him."

"And whose decision was that?" This time there was real anger in his voice. "You could have told me. Not when I was a child, but when I was old enough. You could have told him! You knew when I went to Calpurnia to the university. My mother wrote to you. You could have told him that I was there." He turned, pacing away. "If you had, he could have met me, not as his son but as a promising young man in whom he took an interest. I could have been his protégé like Antisia. All the doors that stayed closed to me because I didn't have any backing would have opened. I would have known him." Bel turned. "But you made the decision not to tell either one of us. It would have interfered with your plan."

To her horror, her voice choked. "It is your destiny!"

"I don't believe in destiny. I believe in choice." His face was closed. "You took the choices away from both of us. You're trying to take the choices away from everyone on Lono about how they live in decades to come."

"Bel, you don't understand the political situation…"

"I understand that they have the right to choose for themselves. Some of those choices will be bad. I give you that. Some islands will choose laws I don't agree with. But they have the right to choose for themselves, not have me choose for them based on what I think they should do."

"Bel, the Innocent…"

"The Innocent will have full voting rights here and on the other islands where they've settled. Tranquility and the other islands will have to deal with that. But the Innocent are going to have to deal with everybody else too. They were refugees a hundred and fifty years ago, absolutely. But it's time to stop trading off that. Nobody living was oppressed on Inanna. They've got to learn to live with their neighbors and elect leaders that represent their interests, not be a protected class that the law doesn't apply to." He paced around the table. "During the transition, they're still under Calpurnian law. Frankly I'd be shocked if

Tranquility didn't adopt some version of Calpurnian law permanently. People may want independence, but they work in the shipyards and industrial parks and the last thing they want is to live by the Compact and subsistence fishing. Some strict interpretationists in the outlying islands may want that and ban all technology, but their sons and daughters are going to hustle out to the big city the first chance they get. People get to choose."

"This is going to be madness," Sura managed. "You can't decide this."

"Can't I?" Bel's eyebrow rose. "What did you think your Blameless Prince would do?" She was silent. "Just be your mouthpiece? You have the crown. I give it into the keeping of the Shrine, a historical artifact of immense value. Remember, you said I could keep whatever else I got along the way." He stepped toward the door. "I've got some other appointments. So you'd best take the crown and go."

Numbly, she picked up the case. "Bel, I want you to know…" Sura began.

"I don't really want to hear that right now," Bel said. "There may be a point in the future when we talk, but it's not today. Goodbye."

The door closed behind her, her heart heavier in her chest than the crown in her hands.

BEL WAS SITTING at the desk, a cup of cold Menaechman coffee at his elbow, staring at the messages on his screen without really seeing them, when the aide buzzed him. "Captain Melian is here to see you."

"Send her in," Bel said. He sat up, rubbing his eyes.

Aurore came slouching in, still wearing her plain black cargo pants. "Do you have a headache all the time?"

"It seems like it," Bel said, straightening. "Join me for coffee?"

"Do you mind if I have mine warm?" she asked with a glance at his sad cup.

"I'll call for another service," Bel said, and did so. Aurore sat down in the visitor's chair. "I just gave the Solaste Crown to Sura."

"Bet that was fun," Aurore said.

"Am I doing the right thing?"

She spread her hands. "I don't know. We can't know. We just do our best." She leaned back. "But there are people alive today who would be dead if we'd made other choices, so that looks like winning to me."

"You have a point," Bel said. He glanced at the screen. "I've got twenty messages from the Innocent fitters. I'm guaranteeing their rights while I rule, but all possible future democratically elected governments aren't something I can control."

"Except by autocracy," Aurore pointed out.

"Except that way, yes." Bel pinched the bridge of his nose. "Calpurnia flattened Inanna. That seems to be where this started. The Internal Wars started right after the Just War and the interdict on Inanna. We leveled their cities and prohibited any kind of large settlement or industrial development. There's nothing there now."

"I don't think that's actually true," Aurore said thoughtfully. "I met an Inannan trade representative. She was a guest of my father's. She helped my father's gaura rescue my brother when he was kidnapped by Altissimus Cassian, which is a long story. Anyway, she was my father's guest for a while after, and she was working out some kind of trade deal for Inanna." She looked apologetic. "I was there briefly when *Golden Wanderer* was in port and stayed in the House, but I was frankly more interested in arming the merchant ships than the trade thing. I said, 'it's nice to meet you' and never had a conversation with her. My eyes glaze over when people start talking about that stuff. But there are still people on Inanna and they want to trade."

"Good to know," Bel said. Of course Aurore knew somebody. They were a great team. There was a time to lay your cards on the table. "Listen, this is a weird job. Everything about it is off-kilter. But if I'm going to keep playing, I'd like to have you in the game. It was your idea that saved the ships and you've got a superlatively smooth bluff. How about staying for a while longer? If I'm going to claim Iulus' Senate seat and be Viceroy of Lono for as long as it takes, I need you with me. How would you like to keep command permanently?"

"You only had to ask." Her dark eyes were bright. "You're going to be the Autarch's heir for real?"

"It's a one in a million chance," Bel said. "And it so happens I'm a gambling man."

The aide buzzed in again. "Altissimus, Altissima Antisia is here as you requested."

Bel glanced at Aurore. "Send her in," he said, and stood up, straightening his collar. "Altissima."

Antisia looked pale, her red uniform stark as blood against her skin, but she met his eyes directly as she entered. "You were right and I was wrong. I'm glad your plan worked. My crew…"

"…is still alive," Bel said. "And so are we all."

She took a deep breath. "What happens now?"

"Now I accept your resignation," Bel said.

"I'm not offering it. I can't." Antisia frowned. "I know my duty. I have to see this through to the bitter end."

"That's not possible for two reasons," Bel said. "First, as long as you're here I look like your puppet. It appears that the Federationist faction has cooked up some imposter to pretend to be Nereus Iulus. You're too strongly associated with the Autarch and you will be presumed to be in command. Second," his voice dropped, "you don't really want to do this. You're done."

"You don't understand," Antisia said. "All my life, since I was a tiny child, this has been everything! The Navy is everything. I can't be done. There is no done. This is my life until the day I die."

"You are done," Bel said gently. "You got your ships out of the defeat at Morrigan. You got your crews safely to Lono. You obeyed the Autarch's last orders. And now you are done. The rest of your life is yours to do something else with. I am accepting your resignation. You do not have a choice."

She blinked twice, green eyes searching his face, her own oddly blank. "Understood, Altissimus." She turned and walked away, stiffly as if her limbs were half-frozen.

Bel waited until the door closed behind her. He sighed.

"That was harsh," Aurore observed.

"She wouldn't have done it herself," he replied. "Just like she wouldn't have followed my order not to make the suicide attack. I can't have suicidal commanders."

"I see that," Aurore said.

"But more than that…" He tried to put it into words someone from

Menaechmi could understand. He understood all too well. He'd learned what he couldn't do at the university. "...the yoke of duty, of gravitas... She can't give that up unless someone makes her. Not even if it's killing her to do it. So I made her."

"What will she do now?" Aurore asked.

"I don't know. That's up to her. And it's probably the first choice she's ever had in her life." He leaned back against the desk, the weight of it suddenly catching up to him. "It's what she needs. It's what Calpurnia needs. What I don't see yet is how to give us those choices."

"Maybe Lono is enough for today," Aurore said.

"Yeah," Bel said, "Maybe so." He shook his head. "I don't know how I'm going to get used to this."

"it's not what you want either," she said.

"No and yes," Bel said slowly. "When I went to Calpurnia to the university I had big dreams. I thought I could change things. That I could be somebody, sure, but also that I could reform and reorganize and make it a better place. I learned really quickly that there was nothing I could do. I was a grant student from the Adelpha Rim and I was competing with patrician kids who'd been coached for this from the time they were three or four, kids like Antisia. They had senatorial parents or patronage connections or they'd done at ten the work I was doing at sixteen. I was welcome to play along and go back to Adelpha when I was finished, but I was never going to be in a position to have a job that would lead anywhere on Calpurnia. And I didn't have the temperament."

"You seem pretty solid to me," Aurore said with a little quirk of her lips.

"Not really." Bel looked up at the ceiling, its ornamented panels glowing with light and color. "So I decided I'd be a supportive partner. I had a girlfriend who was ambitious and smart and better connected. I figured I'd be her backup and help her get where she was going. But when I suggested we get married..." He shrugged. "...she said I was crazy. We were too young. We weren't anything like thirty-five. And she didn't want someone who put her career first. She wanted a go-getter who was better connected than she was and even more ambitious. Not a guy who wears flowered shirts." Bel gestured at his shirt.

Aurore looked confused. "What's wrong with your shirt?"

"It's plebian," Bel said. "It has flowers. And colors. Purple and blue and pink. It doesn't have gravitas."

"You mean it's slightly hapalos," Aurore said.

"Kind of. If by that you mean feminine. Anything feminine is lacking gravitas. It's plebian. Patricians don't wear flowered shirts. So she broke up with me."

"Over your shirt?"

"Pretty much." Bel shrugged. "So I dropped out and went to Lono. Tried being a revolutionary. But I'm not an assassin, so you know how that ended."

Aurore looked thoughtful. "So you wanted to make a difference on Calpurnia and now you can."

"Now I can." He'd said too much, but Aurore seemed like she understood. "Now I have the chance I wanted ten years ago, only I'm a lot wiser than I was when I was at the university."

"Maybe this is what was meant to be," she said.

"I don't believe in destiny," he said. "But I have a chance almost nobody else has. And I've got it in my flowered shirt."

"Well, let's hope it works out better this time," Aurore said with that beautiful smile.

"It's looking good so far," Bel said.

Victoria Antisia was sitting on the bench in the garden under one of the bare trees. In the beds around the statue of the Lord of the Dance, the green stems of some early spring flowers were pushing out of the earth, reaching toward the watery late afternoon sunlight. She'd never learned their names. She sat perfectly still on a bench in the sun.

"Hey." Dian sat down beside her. "Are you speaking to me?"

Victoria looked at her. More than anything, she wished she had a drink. "Why wouldn't I be?"

"Because I helped relieve you of your command," Dian said.

"It had to be," Victoria said. She looked away at the statue, unyielding and uncaring as any work of art. "I've lost it. I don't have it anymore. I'm wrecked. Like some broken piece of equipment. Like the ships that aren't worth repairing."

"Worth it to who?"

She shrugged. "To anyone. I don't function anymore. I fell off the course."

"Maybe you have a worth outside of your social function."

Victoria tilted her head back. "I can't even begin to parse that."

"Come to Menaechmi."

She looked at Dian then. She had dark circles under her eyes, her blue-tipped hair pulled back with a gold clip with honeybees on it that matched the broad bracelet on her wrist. "And do what?"

"I don't know." Dian pursed her lips in that sideways smile. "But you've got plenty of time to find out." She leaned back on the bench. "You can just be Victoria. It's better if Altissima Antisia disappears for a while anyway. You're my guest, a Calpurnian who wanted to leave Lono given the rebellion and all. Nobody's going to think that's weird. As long as you stay off the nets, nobody on Menaechmi is going to know who you are. Come to Beira. Have a vacation."

"I have never had a vacation in my life."

"I believe that," Dian laughed. "So you're going to have one now. Is it really that hard a choice? Death or Dian?"

"If you put it like that, it's no choice at all." She couldn't help smiling. What was it about Dian that made the most absurd things seem reasonable?

"I'm glad I look better than death." Her smile faded. "Seriously, no pressure. We can just be friends if you want. But come to Beira."

"I'd like to be more than friends." That at least she was certain of. To fall into that heady warmth seemed the only soft landing she could imagine.

"Then have an escapade," Dian said. "What have you got to lose?"

"I'll come," she said, and felt a strange weight lift.

"Then let's pack," Dian said. "*Golden Wanderer* is going to be one of the first ships off as soon as Bel gets the hulks out of the way and merchant traffic can go. We'll be home tomorrow."

"Home."

"We'll sit in that double lounger under the jasmine arch and have a drink and watch the stars come out over Beira."

"Yes," Victoria said.

Night had come, but Tranquility Yards was lit brightly as day, white spotlights shining down on the berth where *Golden Wanderer* rested, a cradle tow waiting to be hooked up to pull it out to the launch pads. Aurore ran her hand over the curve of its lower surface. Her crew would take it home safely. Bel had given launch priority, so it would probably be the first ship making planetfall on Menaechmi with news of the Rising on Lono, something her father would find politically advantageous.

Dian came down the ramp, her blue-tipped hair pulled back in a ponytail, her blue velvet pants Dian's idea of suitable for star travel. "Talking to the ship?"

"Just a little," Aurore said. "Make sure to call Dad on an encrypted transmission the minute you come out of jump. You'll have two hours or more in the system run-in before you land and passengers start calling everybody in the world. So however long you have is how long Dad has to make exclusive deals before everybody knows everything he does."

"I've got it, I've got it," Dian said. "Commodities prices. But that's not the big news."

"Just give him your best report. Let him figure out what the political situation means for prices."

Dian put her hands on her hips. "I'm not talking about that. I'm talking about you. It's not very nice of you to leave it to me to tell him, 'Oh wow, I lost my sister! She decided to stay on Lono and captain a warship, so I guess she's probably ok unless she gets killed doing something that I have no idea what.'"

"I can't very well tell him myself," Aurore said.

"You could record a message."

"Saying what?"

"Hi Dad, I decided to join the Lonoi Navy?" Dian said. "Instead of dropping it on me."

"You'll do a better job of explaining," Aurore said.

"Now you're flattering me." Dian smiled archly. "I'll think of something."

Aurore changed the subject. "Is Antisia aboard?"

"Yes. We've got a full load of passengers but I've put her in my cabin. As far as anyone aboard knows, she's a Calpurnian friend of mine who wants to get offworld like about ten thousand other people. Altissima Antisia is a prisoner of Bel's. Victoria is a common name. She can just disappear on Menaechmi for a while."

"Dad will have a stroke," Aurore said.

"Dad will cope." Dian flipped her hair back. "He'll start trying to figure out how to turn it into an advantage. I'm going to make sure she has some space." Her face stilled for a moment. "You be careful. I'm not going to be here to look after you."

"You never do."

"I always do." Dian pulled her in for a solid hug. "Go find that thing you're looking for. That life out there. I'll grow some oranges for you and buy you a drink."

"Yeah," Aurore said. Unexpectedly there were tears in her eyes. She let go. "Good flight."

"Nutty bees," Dian said, and started up the ramp.

Aurore watched the ramp retract, stepping back into the marked zones on the concrete as the tow boss hooked up to *Golden Wanderer* and it started to roll. She walked away. She was all the way back to the end of the yards when she turned around to watch, knowing the tilt of her ship's nose as it eased upright on the distant pad, one green light blinking at its nose. She knew exactly what the comm chatter would be. Dian would be strapped in, all the passengers in their couches waiting for the lift. They'd be getting final clearance. The first officer would give the order for ignition.

And there it was, the blossom of fire beneath as the main engines came online, then the secondaries. *Golden Wanderer* lifted smoothly into the night sky.

"Nutty bees," Aurore said, and she started walking back to *Determination* where it was berthed in the main line.